# Silent Cries for Help 3

*The Finale*

## A Domestic Violence novel by
## Loryn Landon

# Where we left off...

## Grace

## Four Days Later

Malik and I had been talking daily, but we hadn't seen each other outside of work at all this week. Tonight, he was supposed to be coming over and we planned to spend a quiet night alone. Once I finished getting dressed, I headed to work so that I could get my day started. Making it to work, Genie was standing at the reception desk talking to Chantel, as usual. Ever since she and I got into that little spat, she hadn't been saying anything to me and I was fine with that. Making it to my office, I was surprised when I walked in to find two dozen peach colored roses on my desk.

Before I could read the note to see who they were from, Malik walked into my office.

"I hope you like them. I remember you saying that you love all things peach, so I figured I couldn't go wrong with peach colored roses."

"I love them! They are absolutely gorgeous!" I beamed as I rushed into his arms and gave him a big hug and kiss.

1

"You know I love to see that beautiful smile on your face. I promise you that every day I will do everything in my power to keep you smiling like that."

"I appreciate that so much."

"I appreciate you giving me another chance. I swear to you Grace, I promise I won't do anything to ever cause us to fall out again."

"You better not after I done had to damn near fight Chantel over your ass." I chuckled.

We shared a few sensual kisses, which caused a wetness to form between my legs.

"You better stop before I end up laying you across your desk and getting me some of that," he said.

"As good as that sounds, I would hate for someone, especially Kim to come waltzing up in here. We'll have plenty of time tonight for all of that anyway."

"Oh wow! Those are some beautiful flowers." Kim beamed as she walked into my office.

"Thanks Kim."

"Did you get those for her?" she asked Malik.

"Of course, who else would be giving my lady flowers?" he replied full of sarcasm.

It was obvious that Malik wasn't a big fan of Kim and to be honest, she wasn't a big fan of Malik's either. She just tolerated him because he and I were together.

"Oh, stop it silly. We all know that you're the only one." I chuckled, trying to lighten the mood. "I'll see you later. I need to go over the agenda for today with Kim."

"Okay babe," Malik replied, giving me another kiss. "I'll see you later. If you're not too busy we can do lunch."

"I would like that a lot."

After Malik left, Kim sat in the chair by my desk and started laughing.

"That man knows he can have a stank attitude sometimes. I refuse to let him get to me this morning, especially not after the night I had."

"Oh my! Do tell, do tell!" I beamed. "I figured you must have enjoyed yourself when I didn't hear back from you last night."

"Girl, I really did enjoy myself. Thank you so much for hooking me and Andre up. He really is a sweet guy. We hit it off really good. I didn't get into the house until late as hell. Poor Maxi was pissed off at me because she's so used to me going straight home after work. If I would have known that I was going to be out that late, I would have taken her to my mom's house."

"Girl, you and Maxi are a whole vibe. That poor dog doesn't know she's a dog. She's more like a toddler," I said with a chuckle.

"Girl, who you tellin'!"

"I'm so glad you like Andre. I was worried that things would be odd being that he and I met first."

"Girl no! The moment you told me that you weren't into him like that, I was fine with it. If anything, I thought that he was going to feel weird, but he was really cool. We're supposed to be hooking up tomorrow to spend the day at Navy Pier."

"Navy Pier! Oh wow! Good for you. I really hope that things work out between you and him."

"Thanks boo. I see you and Malik are all lovey-dovey. So, things are good huh?" Kim asked.

"Yeah, things are great. We have been talking every night and tonight he is coming over to hang out. It's our first date since we started back talking."

"I'm happy for you. As long as you're happy with it, I'm good with it."

"Thanks Kim, I appreciate that."

Kim and I went over the agenda for the day then she went to her office, leaving me to get to work.

I was so busy that when Malik came and knocked on my office door, I hadn't even realized that half of the day was gone and that it was lunchtime.

"Hey beautiful, you feel like coming up for some air and having a lil lunch with your man?"

"Hey babe, I could really use a break. I hadn't even noticed it was lunchtime."

"Kim got you in here busy as shit." Malik chuckled. "Let's go grab a quick bite to eat. You look like you could use a little break."

Grabbing my purse and cellphone, I logged off of my computer.

"Let me just check in with Kim right quick," I told him, picking up the phone on my desk and calling Kim's extension. "Hey Kim, I'm about to head out with Malik to lunch. I'll be back shortly."

"Okay girl, see you when you get back. I'm waiting for Andre to call me. He should be going on break at work soon."

"Okay girl!" I squealed, causing her to laugh. "I'll talk to you when I get back."

Hanging up with Kim, I locked my arm in Malik's as we headed out my office. Walking past the reception desk with my head held high, it felt good seeing Chantel roll her eyes when she saw us. She rolled her eyes, letting it be known she didn't like it, but she didn't say anything.

"So, what do you have a taste for?" I asked Malik as we walked toward the parking garage.

"You."

"Me?! No silly, what do you want for lunch?"

"I want you."

"We'll have plenty of time for you to taste me tonight. Aren't you hungry?"

"Not for any food. Are you hungry for food?" Malik asked as he got on the elevator at the parking structure to go to the floor he parked on.

Embracing me, he lifted my chin and started kissing me soft and slow. Inserting his tongue into my mouth, we started French kissing and it was turning me on. I had tingles running up and down my spine as my lady part started to throb.

"Are you hungry for food Grace?" he asked again in the most sensual way.

"I mean, I was."

Before we could go back to kissing, the elevator dinged signaling that we were on the level he parked on. Taking my hand, he led me to his truck.

"How about we find somewhere secluded to park and have a nooner?" he requested.

"Have a what?" I laughed.

"A nooner," he repeated.

"What's a nooner?"

"A little afternoon delight."

"Oh okay! I feel you."

I wasn't the type of lady to fool around in a car, but the way I was feeling, I was down for a little rendezvous. He ended up finding a secluded section in the Kraft parking garage and I was nervous.

"What if we get caught?"

"We won't get caught silly. As you can see there is no one in sight."

"I see that, but what if there are cameras?" I asked nervously.

"There aren't any cameras. Stop being a chicken and hop in the back seat."

Doing as he asked, I got out of the truck then got in the back seat. I was nervous yet intrigued. I had never ever done anything as risky as fooling around in a public place.

"You don't have anything to worry about. See how dark my windows are. No one can see in. I promise we're good," he coaxed as he leaned in and started kissing me again.

At that point, I was gone. He slid his pants down then helped me out of my pants and it was on and popping from there. Once he started giving me oral pleasure, I was gone. In that moment, I didn't care if we did get caught. All that mattered was the amazing sensations he had flowing through my body.

## Later That Night

After our little afternoon delight, the rest of the day flew by. Once the day was over, Malik followed me to my house. Making it home, I needed to shower to feel refreshed from our lil nooner or whatever he called it.

"I'll be right back. I'm about to shower and change right quick."

"Okay baby, I'ma order the food then come and join you. Where do you want me to put your flowers?"

"Thank you, babe. You can put them on the living room table. They are so beautiful, I just love them," I replied, giving Malik a kiss.

Sitting my cellphone, keys and purse down on the kitchen counter, I headed to my bathroom so that I could jump in the shower. I was looking forward to spending the evening with him. I couldn't have been happier by how things were going between us.

Taking my clothes off then heading to the bathroom, I turned the shower on then got in. The hot water felt amazing as it cascaded down over my body. Grabbing my mango scented bottle of Dove body wash, I poured some on my washcloth then lathered my body with soap. Paying special attention to my lady parts, I made sure to wash up really good as I thought about Malik giving me some more oral pleasure. Just the thought of it was causing my body to tingle. Rinsing the soap off of the rest of my body, I lathered my washcloth with more soap and repeated lathering my body down washing off.

As soon as I was done rinsing off, I felt a cold draft. Turning around, I saw Malik standing there with the coldest glare in his eyes. Before I could say anything, he reached into the shower and grabbed me by the neck then yanked me out of the shower.

"Malik! Stop it! You're hurting me!" I cried out.

"Why you keep playing with my emotions Grace! Why is that nigga calling you?" he bellowed as he pushed me up against the bathroom wall.

"I can't breathe Malik! Let me go!" I pleaded as I tried to pry his hands from around my neck.

"Answer the fucking question!" he yelled, taking his hands from around my neck and replacing them with his forearm, pinning me against the wall.

"What are you talking about?" I truly had no clue what he was talking about.

"Stop playing fuckin' stupid! Why the FUCK that nigga callin' your phone?!"

The only dude that I could think of that would be calling my phone was Andre.

"Let me go so I can explain," I cried. My feelings were hurt. Just earlier today, he promised me that he wasn't ever going to hurt me and now here he was getting physical with me again.

Letting me go, he took a step back and I walked into my bedroom.

"Answer my fuckin' question Grace! I'm trying not to hurt your ass, but you about to take me there!"

Shit it was too late for that. He had already put his hands on me and hurt me. I didn't know what he meant by me taking him there, but not wanting to find out, I tried to think of who he could be talking about.

"The only guy that has my phone number is a guy name Andre. He's someone that I hooked Kim up with. I can call him back and prove it to you. Let me go get my phone."

Slapping me across the face, he hit so hard that I fell to the ground.

"Get your lyin' ass up and try that shit again! This time don't fuckin' lie to me!"

"I promise I'm not lying to you Malik. The only guy that has my number is a friend of mine named Andre and he is dating Kim. Just let me go get–"

Slapping me again, he raised his fist then held it against my face.

"Why the fuck that nigga Desmond callin' your fuckin' phone?" he bellowed.

"Desmond?! What are you talking about?! Desmond doesn't have my phone number!"

"You think I'm a fuckin' fool!" he yelled, slapping me again, causing me to fall. This time, the side of my head hit the ottoman that was in my room.

Feeling dazed, I laid there crying.

"I swear to you, Desmond doesn't have my number."

"You lyin' ass bitch!"

"I'm not lyin' Malik!"

"Yes, the fuck you are! If Desmond don't have your number, then why the fuck did I just hang up on his simple ass?!" he bellowed as he continued raining punches to my body.

All I could do was curl up and try my best to cover my face as I took all of his blows. The whole time, he was yelling at me. He was calling me names and swearing to God that I was causing him to snap as he hit me over and over again. I continued to lay there as my body burned from the pain that I was in, bracing myself as best as I could from the hits that he kept giving me. When he finally stopped, I slowly put my hands down from covering my face and as soon as I turned around, he punched me square in the face causing me to pass out.

# Chapter 1

## Malik

Pacing the floor back and forth as I occasionally glanced down at Grace as she laid all battered and bruised, I was trying to figure out what to do next. I couldn't believe that she had driven me to the point of snapping out on her ass again. The audacity of her and that nigga Desmond! They had probably been carrying on behind my back this whole damn time!

*I can't believe I fell for another lying ass bitch!*

Looking down at her the cut on her head was bleeding out pretty badly.

"FUCK!" I yelled in frustration.

I had to snap out of my anger mode so that I could think clearly. I wasn't sure if Grace was going to need stitches or not but letting her lay there bleeding out wasn't a good idea. That much I did know.

"Grace! Come on Grace," I snapped trying to get her to wake up.

Kneeling down and holding her in my arms, I tried to shake her hard enough to get her to wake up, but nothing was working. Instantly, panic started to set in.

"GRACE! Now dammit, you need to wake up!" I spat again as I continued to shake her like a rag doll.

She was out cold. If it wasn't for the fact that I could tell she was still breathing I would have felt compelled to call 911. Since she was breathing, I just continued to shake her as I yelled out her name.

"GRACE!!" I yelled out again but all she did was stir a little.

Picking her up, I laid her in her bed then headed to the bathroom to get a washcloth. Running it under some cold water then ringing out the excess water, I headed back into the bedroom and placed the washcloth on her head.

As soon as I laid the washcloth on her head, she began to stir a little more. Hearing her phone ringing in the other room, I left her laying in the bedroom and headed to get her phone to see who was calling her.

Seeing the name, Sabrina, flash across the screen I let the phone ring. I figured if it was important, she could leave Grace a voice message. While I was standing in the kitchen, I checked her call log to see if that nigga had called back. Seeing that he hadn't, I left her phone on her kitchen counter then went to the fridge to find something to drink.

Opening the fridge, I spotted a bottle of Stella Rose mango. It wasn't my usual go-to drink but I needed something to calm my nerves. Pouring myself a glass full then drinking it in one gulp, I poured another glass and downed the second one just as I had done the first one.

I hated to feel like I was being played. Grace thought she was slick talkin' about Desmond didn't have her number, yet I had a whole conversation with him from her fucking phone. The nigga had the nerve to tell me to give Grace the message because it was somewhat urgent and very important that she called him back.

I didn't know what his ass had going on with her that was so urgent and important, but as soon as she came to I planned to ask her and if she lied, she was going to get her ass kicked... again.

Feeling my cellphone vibrating in my back pants pocket, I pulled it out to see who was calling. Seeing that it was Lauren, I hesitated on whether or not I should answer her call. Heading to Grace's bedroom and peeking in, I saw that she was still laying down, but it looked like she was awake. Instead of answering for Lauren, I let the call go to voicemail.

Stepping into the bedroom, I felt my cellphone vibrate again. Pulling it from my pocket I saw that I had a text notification.

**Lauren: Hey sexy, I was hoping to catch you. Wanted to see if you were available to hook up**

**Me: I'm in the middle of something at the moment. I'll hit you back as soon as I get done**

**Lauren: I'll be waiting**

That chick didn't have any chill. Lauren couldn't get enough of my ass and what killed me was the fact that she was trying to play hard to get. She acted like she didn't want to be in a relationship, yet she stayed on my line calling to hook up with a nigga. All that shit she was talking about how she has male friends was probably some bullshit. Lauren struck me as the type of female that liked to play games. She probably had her heart broken in the past and was scared of commitment. I didn't believe for one second that she was out there bad hooking up with different men like she tried to put it.

Seeing that Grace was now awake, I headed further into the room. We still had some shit to discuss and I wasn't leaving until she told me the truth about her and ol' boy. That shit had me really feeling some type of way. When she brought up that dude, Andre talking about he the other guy that could have called her, I needed her to further explain that shit also.

When I left her office earlier, I overheard her and Kim talking about dude and from the sounds of it, he was trying to get with Grace first. I didn't know what type of shit her and Kim had going on, but I was about to find all that shit out.

# Chapter 2

### Desmond

"Uh, hello, is Grace available?"

"Who wants to know?"

"This is Desmond. Is she around by any chance?"

"As a matter of fact, no, she ain't available. What the fuck you calling my girl for?"

"My bad bro, no harm no foul. I'm not calling on nothing disrespectful. I have some important information to discuss with her and was hoping I could speak with her."

"Well, like I said she ain't available."

"Okay, bro, let her Desmond called," I said.

"I ain't yo' bro, nigga!"

"Like I said I don't mean no disres-"

"You disrespected us by picking up the fucking phone and calling my girl."

"Look, it's not what you think. It's urgent that I speak with her..."

"What's so urgent that you need to speak with my lady about?"

"That's between me and her. If she's willing to share that with you that's on her."

"Dude check this... don't call me girl's number again."

"Excuse me?"

"You heard just what the fuck I said. Don't call this number again before I have to come see yo ass!"

CLICK!

I couldn't believe the fool had the nerve to hang the phone up in my face like that. It was already shocking that he had answered Grace's phone to begin with, but to snap out like he did was bogus as hell.

Heading back inside my parents' house, I walked into the kitchen where my dad was sitting looking at WGN news coverage on the old police superintendent getting caught drunk and losing his job. The last thing the city needed was to not have the right leadership or no leadership at all when it came to their police department. Crime in the city was at an all-time high. So much so that you couldn't even go to the city to enjoy any of the attraction spots in fear of getting your life taken.

Seeing my dad sitting at the kitchen table, babysitting a cup of coffee was truly a sight to see. Ever since my mom passed, he had been taking it hard but trying to be strong for the strength of me and Faith. He convinced me to reach out to Grace to not only let her know that my mom passed away, but to tell her about

Faith in hopes that she would be open to wanting to meet her.

My mom's last words of how Faith was going to need her mom in her life were on repeat in my mind, especially now that the funeral was over. I needed to try to get all the support that I could for my baby girl. She was taking my mom's death pretty hard. She was being distant and had been cooped up in her room ever since. Mom passing away had taken a toll on all of us, but I knew that I had to keep going. I didn't want to let her down. It was clear that it weighed heavy on my mom what was going to happen with Faith, as well as all of us once she passed so I wasn't going to stop until I carried her wishes out.

When my dad convinced me to call Grace up, it was in the hopes that Faith meeting Grace would help her deal with the loss of my mom. We weren't trying to replace my mom in Faith's life. We just needed all the help and support that we could get.

"So, how did it go?" my dad asked, breaking me from my thoughts.

"It didn't go good," I mumbled, shaking my head in disappointment.

"Well, what happened? What did she say?"

"Her boyfriend answered her phone and not only was he pissed, but he wouldn't let me talk to Grace. I don't even think he is going to give her the message."

"Boy oh boy."

That was all my dad said.

"I know. I don't even know if I should try calling her back."

"I wouldn't son. Let it be so that things can cool off between them. The last thing you want is to cause her any problems. Just give it a couple of days and check back with her."

"How you feeling, pops?"

"Shit hanging in there as best as I can son. What about you?"

"I just try not to think about it."

"Well, whatever works, you know. Have you talked to Faith?"

"Not since earlier. She's been up in the room with Bear all day."

"Yeah, I went and checked on her while you were outside on the phone and she was in there reading a book."

"That girl know she loves to read."

"I know, she must've gotten that from her mother because it was hell getting you to read when you were younger." My dad chuckled, causing me to laugh with him.

Even though we both were hurting and grieving, he still had his sense of humor.

"I just never was the book type. Are you hungry? What do you have a taste for?"

"Well, we usually have pizza on Fridays. But if you want something else that is fine. It doesn't matter to me."

"Maybe I will check with Faith to see what she wants."

"Yeah, that would be good."

Leaving my dad in the kitchen, I headed upstairs to Faith's room. As I made it to her door, I couldn't help but to stop and look toward my parents' bedroom. The last time I was in their room was the day my mom had passed away.

Being that she passed away in their bed, the next day, I went out and got my dad a new bed. I had offered to set up the spare room that was made into a small sitting room upstairs for my dad, thinking he wouldn't want to sleep in his room, but he was adamant on sleeping in his own room.

He told me that he couldn't handle sleeping on the bed that my mom had passed away in, but there was no other room in the house that he wanted to switch to. He said that I should be more afraid of the living and not the dead and that my mom's presence in their room was what kept him sane.

I didn't understand it, but if it worked for him then it worked for me. I still felt very uncomfortable being near their room. I was going to need more time and I was grateful that the room I was staying in was in the basement.

I ended up moving into my parents' house temporarily and I offered Lexi to stay in my townhouse, but she said that she was good living with her mom and that she was looking forward to her mom being able to help her once our son came. So, at the moment, I was still paying the rent on my place while trying to decide what to do for the long run with it.

"Knock, knock... can I come in sweetie?"

"Hey Dessy," Faith said.

She was sitting in the middle of her bed reading a book with Bear on her lap.

"How are you feeling baby girl?"

"Mmmmm, I'm okay," she responded, not even looking up from her book. I could tell that she wasn't as okay as she was trying to portray.

"Do you want to talk about it?"

"Nope."

"Are you hungry?"

"Mmmmm, a little."

"What do you have a taste for?"

"I don't know," Faith responded still looking in her book.

"Hey, can you look at me when I'm speaking to you please?" I asked, reaching for her book and easing her hands down from her face. "You know you can talk to me about anything right?"

"I know Dessy. But I don't want to talk about anything right now."

"Okay, well will you promise me that if you do want to talk you will let me know."

"Sure."

I felt so bad. I didn't know what to do. Being a parent was a first for me because my mom and dad held those roles down. Even after we told Faith that I was her dad, I still had my mom's support. But now that she was gone, I had to jump in parent mode with a 10-year-old girl and I didn't have a clue what to do or say. All I knew how to do was to comfort her as well as give her some space.

"I need your help with something Faithy. I'm trying to figure out what to cook for dinner. Do you have any ideas?" I asked hoping to get her to open up just a little.

"Uh, do you have to cook, or can we order some food?"

"I was thinking about cooking," I lied, I wasn't the best cook so there was no way I was going to even attempt to cook dinner for us all.

"Uh Dessy do you even know how to cook?"

"Uh excuse me!" I said sarcastically causing Faith to laugh.

That was my goal. To put a smile on her face and the bonus was to make her laugh.

"You tryna say I can't cook?"

"Nooooo!" Faith laughed. "I just never seen you cook."

"Well, I know how to make some really good ramen noodles and my peanut butter and jelly sandwiches are the best."

"I don't know if that is a good idea." Faith laughed. "Plus, daddy... I mean poppa," she paused trying to find the correct term to use for my dad. Being that she had always called him dad, and now knowing I was her dad, I could tell she was trying to be considerate.

"You can call poppa 'dad' if you feel comfortable Faithy. I know all of this is very new to you sweetie. How about I order us some pizza? How does that sound?"

"That sounds much better than noodles and peanut butter and jelly," she said with a laugh. "Dessy, if I call poppa daddy still, then what should I call you?"

"You can call me whatever you feel comfortable calling me. So, if you are comfortable calling me Dessy, then Dessy is fine with me baby girl."

Giving her a big hug, I couldn't stop the lone tear that escaped my eye. My baby girl had been faced with so much over the last few weeks. In that moment, I realized that even though she had said that she was okay with the adoption, it was clear that she was struggling with handling it. Faith was a sweet and caring little girl that was much wiser than her age, so I knew she was holding back her true feelings in fear of upsetting me and my dad.

"Can you get sausage and pepperoni with mushrooms and onions?"

"Geesh, you want all of that on the pizza?!"

"Yeah, it's really good. And can you get me a slice of strawberry cheesecake if you order from that Giordano's place?"

"Of course, sweetie. Is there anything else you would like for me to get?"

"No." Faith giggled.

"Okay, I'ma go order it now."

"Dessy, can I ask you a question?"

"Sure sweetie, what's up?"

"Have you gotten in contact with Grace yet?"

Hearing Faith ask me about Grace made my heart hit my stomach.

"Uh, not yet sweetie. As soon as I reach her, I will let you know... okay?"

"Okay, thank you Dessy."

"Sure thing, sweetie."

Stepping out of Faith's room I headed straight for the bathroom that was across the hall from her room.

Standing in the bathroom and looking into the mirror, I had to take a couple of deep breaths. Turning the water on, I cleaned my face and just as I finished, my cellphone started ringing.

Taking a hand towel that was hanging on a rack in the bathroom, I dried my hands and face then pulled my phone out to see who was calling. Seeing that it was Lexi calling, I answered.

"Hey Lex, you good?"

"No," she answered as she breathed heavily. "I'm in labor. I need you to meet me at the hospital. I'm on my way now. Leave now Desmond!"

# Chapter 3

## Grace

"GRACE! Now dammit, you need to wake up!"

I heard Malik yelling as I laid still. He was shaking me by the shoulders trying to get me to wake up and although I heard him, I played like I didn't. For one, the pain that was running through my body, as well as in my head, made it hard for me to just wake up. For two, I didn't want Malik to continue to hit on me.

I couldn't believe he had jumped on me like he did. What Kim had said about men hitting you and it getting worst each time was every bit of the truth. The last time he put his hands on me he had punched me in the face. But this time, he beat my ass as if I was a nigga off the street. I never saw that coming especially since we were having such a good day.

I figured that if I played possum, he would just leave me be. Feeling him pick me up off the floor, and lay me in the bed, it felt like my heart was going to beat out of my chest. I was nervous and scared to death. I didn't know what he was going to do. Then I heard him in the bathroom running water, so I peeked through one of my eyes to see what it was that he was doing.

The light in the bedroom instantly caused a pain to shoot across my head. I wanted so badly to reach up and hold the spot on my head that was throbbing in pain, but I didn't want Malik to know that I was awake just yet. Seeing him head back toward me with what looked like a washcloth in his hand, I closed my eyes and tried my best to lay as still as I could.

"Grace!"

I heard Malik say as he placed a cool rag across my forehead. The coolness from the washcloth gave me a little relief from the burning and aching pain that I was feeling in that spot.

Still lying still, I prayed that he would just leave me alone so that I could try to get up and assess the damage that he had done to my body. I knew this time around it was going to be bad because he had punched me all over my body.

When he walked out of the room, I lifted the washcloth and saw that there was blood on it. I wasn't sure if that was from falling and hitting my head on the ottoman or from him raining punches on my face. Either way, I was upset nonetheless that he had beat my ass like he had.

The few minutes that he left me alone in the bedroom, I couldn't do anything but silently cry. I was in so much pain both mentally and physically. I hated the fact that I had let Malik back into my life just for him to do the very thing to me that he said he would never do again. I wanted to cry out for help, but I didn't want to risk pissing him off again, thinking that the ass kicking he had given me was over.

Remembering that he said Desmond had called me had me wondering if he was telling me the truth or not. I had seen Desmond a handful of times since I moved back to town, but we had never exchanged numbers. I was totally blown away and lost when Malik said that he had talked to Desmond on my phone.

With Malik lying to me and turning into a monster in a matter of seconds like he had done had me confused. I didn't know what to think. He promised to never hurt me again, and he lied about that. Who's to say that he wasn't lying about Desmond calling my phone! I couldn't help but to think about the situation with him and Chantel and how she was so angry and jealous of me and Malik. Instantly, I felt like another fool. Maybe Chantel was right. Maybe everything that she had said about Malik was right and in some sick way, she was trying to look out for me. Just earlier today, I was walking past her with my head held high on Malik's arm, when I really should have let her have him.

My thoughts were quickly interrupted when Malik walked back into the room. All I could do was think,

*Lord, please don't let this man hit me again. I'm not sure how much more my body can take.*

"I need you to get up Grace."

I knew that he had seen me stirring and moving around, so I couldn't play like I was still out.

"I'm in pain from you hitting on me Malik. I can barely move, and my head is pounding."

"That ain't all that is going to be pounding if you don't get your ass up!" Malik demanded.

"Why can't you just leave Malik?" I began to plead. "Please, just leave me alone. I don't know what I could have done to deserve this-"

Grabbing me by the throat and forcing me into a sitting position, he glared into my eyes. He had his hands tightly around my neck, but not tight enough where I couldn't breathe. I was thankful for that, yet afraid at what he was going to do next.

"Please stop! You're hurting me. You said you would never hurt me again."

"That was before you lied to me!" Malik growled.

"But I didn't lie to you. I swear I didn't!"

"Yes, the fuck you did!" he screamed, grabbing my throat tighter causing me to start gagging and choking.

"Please... Malik... I can't breathe!" I cried.

Releasing the chokehold that he had on my neck, I instantly grabbed my neck trying to shake the soreness that was left behind from him choking me.

"I'ma ask you one last time Grace. If you lie to me, I promise you shit ain't going to be good for you. I'ma go to jail tonight and I put that on my momma if you fuckin' lie! You hear me?!"

Shaking my head yes, he continued to yell in my face.

"Do you fuckin' hear me talking to you?!" Shaking my head, he went to grab me, and I flinched. "Then fuckin' say it!"

"I hear you Malik..." I tried to say as clearly as I could with my neck being sore.

"Now, why the FUCK did that nigga call your phone and if you say you don't know, I'ma catch me a fuckin' body tonight! I swear to fuckin' God I am."

"Malik, I won't lie," I promised, I was shaking because I didn't know what the hell he wanted me to say. I didn't know how Desmond got my number. I took a deep breath, hurting my sore throat in the process and continued. "Desmond and I have a history. but I swear on my life I didn't give him my number. I'm thinking someone that knows me that knows him must have given my number to him."

"Someone like who? And what exactly is so fuckin' important that he needs to speak to you about? You been fuckin' on this nigga Grace?"

"NO! No! I haven't seen him since we were at Wildfire that day."

"So, what's so fuckin' important between y'all?"

"I'm not sure," I began, and his eyes turned ice cold. I knew in that moment; shit wasn't about to be good for me. "He and I went through something very traumatic when we were younger," I started explaining. "But that was over 10 years ago. I have no idea what he needs to talk to me about. You can check my phone. I guarantee you there are no other calls with whatever number he called from in my phone."

"I ain't checking shit so you can send me off again. Who's to say you ain't delete the shit."

"Why would I delete it? Check my phone Malik. I have nothing to hide from you," I cried. "I swear to God, I'm not lying to you."

"Yeah, sure you don't. From what I can see, you are one sneaky ass female. You know you're a fuckin' liar Grace! You play the role like you all innocent and shit, but ya ass ain't shit."

"Malik, I don't have a reason to lie to you."

"How do I know that?! Huh? How the fuck do I know that you ain't try to get that old thang back with dude?! Especially since you sit up and listen to all the bullshit Chantel be telling ya ass. Hell, if you think I have been dishonest with you about her, who's to say you wouldn't try to hook up with dude?!"

"I can't hook up with him if I don't have a way too," I pleaded.

"Didn't I just tell you he called your phone?" he bellowed, pushing me off the bed.

"Malik stop it! Please!" I said as I hit the floor.

"Didn't I just tell your ass that I talked to the fuckin' nigga on your phone?" he continued as he reached down and grabbed me, picking me up off of the floor.

Barely able to stand as my body was riddled in pain, I did my best to not make any sudden moves. I remember from the first fight that he used me hitting him first as an excuse for punching me like he did.

"So, you gon' just stand there and act like you don't hear me talking to you!"

"I hear you Malik. I just don't know what to say."

"You can start with telling me what the fuck is so important that the nigga gotta talk to you!"

"I don't know!" I cried out. "I swear to God, we haven't spoken in over 10 years."

"You lyin' bitch!" he yelled as he hauled off and slapped me in the mouth.

Instantly, I felt a stinging sensation along with the metallic taste of blood.

"Malik! Stop!" I screamed and it was like he was in a trance.

I continued to scream for him to stop at the top of my lungs as he continued to yell back at me calling me a liar. Crying out for help, I prayed that someone would hear what was going on and send me some help.

Feeling myself getting dizzy, I stumbled to the ground, falling to my knees. All I could do was ball up and pray that he wouldn't hit me again as I continued to cry wondering what I had done to deserve this.

Thankfully, Malik didn't put his hands on me, but he continued to yell at me, calling me names while cursing me out. One of my neighbors must have heard enough of what was going on because all of a sudden there was loud knocking on the door.

"Fuck! You keepin' up all that noise disturbing the peace. Shit! You betta hope it's not the police!"

All I could think to myself was Lord, please let it be the police because that was probably the only way I would be able to get Malik to leave.

"I'ma go open the door. If you make so much as a fuckin' peep I promise you I will kill you. Understood!?"

Shaking my head yes, I did my best to brace myself so that I could sit up. While he left to go answer the door, I used the side of my bed as a crutch to help me stand up from the floor. As I slowly walked toward the bathroom, I saw a good bit of blood on my carpet by my bed thinking to myself that must have come from my head when I hit it and fell. Making it to the bathroom I looked up in the mirror and instantly felt sick to my stomach at the sight that was staring back at me.

# Chapter 4

## Malik

"Who is it?" I asked as I walked up to Grace's front door.

Whoever it was they were impatient as hell, banging and knocking on Grace's fucking door like they were insane. All I could think was that one of her nosey as neighbors had done called the police because of all the screaming Grace's ass was doing.

"It's John, I live next door."

Opening the door, I gave John the glance over. He was a middle- aged white man that looked a lot like Bruce Willis.

"Is there something I can help you with, John?"

"I heard a lot of yelling, screaming and banging around. I just wanted to make sure that everything was okay. Is the young lady that lives here okay?"

"Yes, that young lady that you are speaking of is my girl and she is just fine, thank you! All you heard were two people, in love, having some very hard and ruff sex."

"Oh, well... it sounded like a little more than just sex."

"How 'bout you mind your fuckin' business John. Everything is fine here. You can go on home now."

Closing the door in his face before he could say anything else, I couldn't do anything but shake my head. Heading back into the bedroom, I noticed that Grace was nowhere in sight. Peeping that she was in the bathroom with the door closed I went to go open it.

"Why you close the door?"

"I just wanted some privacy Malik. Who was at the door?"

I noticed that I had really snapped out and done a number on her this time. She had a nasty looking gash on the side of her forehead, one of her eyes were red and swollen, her lip was busted, and the side of her face was red with my handprint across it. There for a second, I felt bad for flashing out on her like that, but the way that my adrenaline was running from that nigga calling her phone took me over the edge.

Everything that Grace was trying to hold over my head when it came to Chantel, she was doing the exact same thing and it was pissing me off. She felt a way about me not telling her about Chantel, but she was keeping secrets from me about her and ol' boy. She was a fuckin' trip and if she didn't get her act together, she was going to have me seriously hurt her ass.

I tried my best to not let this side of myself surface, but Grace had a way of bringing the best as well as the worst out of me. Then with all the screaming she was doing, being all over dramatic and shit, she caused for one of her nosey ass neighbors to come to the fuckin' door calling himself checking on her. It was like she was trying to get me caught up or something.

"It was one of your nosey ass neighbors. With all the hoopin' and hollerin' your ass up in here doing, you done got the folks next door all up in our business. Ain't no tellin' who else heard you actin' the fool."

"I think I need stitches Malik. I can't get the cut on my head to stop bleeding," Grace responded, not even acknowledging what I had just said.

She was so selfish that she didn't even attempt to apologize to me for making such a ruckus that folks were minding our business.

"Damn, it does look pretty deep," I agreed as I inspected the wound.

"Can you please leave so that I can go to the hospital to get it check out?"

"Oh, hell na! You must think I'm stupid. Nah, I will take you to the hospital."

"I would rather take myself."

"Not going to happen. Your neighbor already probably sitting by his door calling the police wit his nosey ass. I guess you wanna lie to me and say you going to the hospital when you probably planning to go to the police instead."

"I'm not going to the police Malik. This cut is really bad," she replied as she rinsed out the washcloth she was using, then applied it to her forehead. "If you think that my neighbor is calling the police then you should probably leave... unless you want the police to catch you here."

"Well, if the police show up, tell them that I'm your friend. Matter of fact, that's going to be the exact same thing you gone tell those folks at the hospital too. The last thing that I need is for the law to be all up in my business. Do you understand me Grace?"

She stood there looking at me like I had a third eye.

"Did you not understand what I just told you? Had you kept things real with me about you and ol' boy from the jump, none of this would have ever happened."

"Yes Malik. I understood what you said."

"Good, now you should get yourself cleaned up so that you can go get sewed up. I'll be back later to check on you."

Grace slowly walked pass me as she headed into her room to get dressed. Gathering my things, I broke the silence that was lingering before I walked out.

"I'm serious Grace, this stays between us. If you get the law involved the consequences are going to get very serious."

"Okay Malik," she mumbled as she started to get dressed. She was crying and sniffling... the shit was working my nerves.

"And cut all the crying out! None of this would have happened if you would have kept shit real with me. You make me wonder why I even bother fuckin' with yo ass. Not only are you gullible, sneaky, and a liar, but yo ass a crybaby too. You really need to get your shit together if you ever plan on getting and keeping a good man in your life Grace. Real talk!"

I spat a little knowledge to her on my way out of her room as I headed out of her apartment. Leaving out her front door, I was relieved that the police wasn't outside waiting on me. I was sure that her Bruce Willis lookin' ass neighbor called the law. The last thing that I needed was to catch another domestic violence case.

In my last serious relationship, my ex brought the worst out of me every chance that she got. As a result, I damn near had to whoop her ass on a daily. A few times, things got out of hand and the police had to be called. I had even gone to jail a couple of times behind her ass. When it got to the point that I almost lost my job at Kraft, I had to leave her ass alone. Now, here I was having to deal with the same shit, not only with Grace, but with Chantel.

Remembering that Lauren had reached out wanting to hook up, I figured I would head over to her crib so that I could release some pent- up frustration that Grace had caused. I needed the type of distraction that I knew she would be willing to give at this moment.

# Chapter 5

### Desmond

"Hey dad, I gotta go. Lexi just called talking about she is in labor."

"Say what! Hold up, let me get my hat so I can come with you."

"You don't have to. I was actually going to order a pizza, and have it delivered because Faith is looking forward to having pizza tonight. I don't want to throw her night off having to sit up in the hospital."

"Oh nonsense. If that girl is about to have your child, we should be there to support you."

"That's the thing. Lexi is so dramatic I need to make sure that it is in fact labor and not those Braxton Hicks things she was just having the other day. The baby isn't due for another three weeks."

"Oh okay, you sure son?"

"I'm positive dad. The pizza will be here shortly." I had just ordered the pizza on the app I had installed on my phone. "Once I get there, I will call to give you an update. If she is really in labor, I'll call you so you and Faith can head up to the hospital."

"Okay, that's cool with me. Good luck son. That Lexi chick sure is a handful. I don't know what you were thinking having a baby with her." My dad chuckled reminding me of my mom.

She could not stand Lexi and with good reason.

"I know dad. This baby was not planned at all. But I am excited to be having a son."

"I get it. Make sure to keep me posted."

Giving my dad a hug, which was something that was starting to become normal instead of giving him dap and walking off, I grabbed my keys so that I could head out and get to the hospital. The last thing that I needed was for Lexi to really be in labor and I wasn't there. I would never hear the end of it.

Once I got in my car and was heading toward the hospital, I thought I should have let Faith know what was going on. But then again, if it was a false alarm, I didn't want to get her hopes up.

Surprisingly, there wasn't much traffic, so I was making pretty good time heading toward the hospital. Worried about Lexi and the baby was a given, but I also couldn't shake the feelings of being worried about Grace.

I was taken off guard by how rude her dude was. I hoped that I hadn't caused her any problems by calling her. I was under the impression that I was calling her cellphone, but I guess Sabrina didn't make it clear to my dad if that was Grace's house phone or cell number. Either way, I wasn't expecting for a dude to answer. I wondered if it was the dude that I saw her at the restaurant with. Either way, he came across as a punk.

Pulling into the emergency parking lot, I was thankful to find a spot that was not too far from the entrance. Lexi didn't give me any specific directions other than to meet her at the hospital, so I expected that she would be at the emergency entrance instead of the main entrance, since she was having an emergency and all.

Heading inside, I glanced around the room to see if I saw Lexi or her mom. Not seeing neither one of them, I headed to the front desk where two nurses sat checking in people.

"Hi sir, do you need to be seen by a doctor?"

"Uh no ma'am. I'm checking to see if..." I had to pause for a minute because Lexi wasn't my girlfriend and I felt weird saying baby momma, although that was exactly what she was. "I wanted to know if Alexis Jackson checked in yet."

"Who are you to the patient?"

"She is pregnant with my son. She told me to meet her here because she suspects she is in labor."

"Okay, hold on let me check for you. What did you say your name was?" the male nurse asked. It was obvious that he had a lot of sugar in his tank. I couldn't do anything but chuckle at how animated he was acting.

"Desmond Holloway."

The nurse typed something into the computer then looked up at me.

"She hasn't checked in yet sir. But if she is in labor, she could be at Labor and Delivery. Let me call over there for you to check to see if she checked in over there."

"Okay thanks, I appreciate that."

I had no idea that there was a labor and delivery department. Lexi didn't mention anything like that to me when she called. She just said for me to meet her at the hospital. I stood off to the side as I waited for him to call and check to see if Lexi was over there.

"Okay sir, she is over in the Labor and Delivery department. Let me give you the directions to get over there."

As the nurse explained how to get to labor and delivery, I felt my phone vibrating in my pocket. Once he was done, I pulled my phone out as I headed out of the emergency department. Seeing that it was Lexi calling, I answered.

"Desmond, where are you? You should have been here by now!" Lexi spat before I could even say anything.

Reaching the emergency room door, just as I was about to open the door, I noticed two women walking in. Being the gentleman that I was, I held the door opened for them as I responded to Lexi.

"I'm here at the hospital. I'm in the Emergency Department. You never said anything about labor and... Lexi I'll be on my way."

Hanging up, I cut the conversation with Lexi short seeing that one of the women that was walking into the door was Grace. It looked like she had gotten attacked something serious. Instantly, a rush of anger and pain shot through my body for her. I knew that I needed to head over to Lexi, but I just needed to find out if Grace was okay and what exactly happened to her.

"Grace!" I muttered as she walked through the door. "Oh my God! Grace what happened to you?" I asked as I followed her toward the emergency room check-in.

She didn't answer. She just held her head down as sped up.

"Grace! What happened to you?"

"Her crazy ass fuckin' no good ass boyfriend put his dick beaters on her!" the lady that was with Grace answered.

Grace stopped walking just shy of the check-in desk.

"Excuse ma'am, but what did you say? Did you say her boyfriend did this to her?"

"Sorry Grace but I'ma tell it," the lady replied. "Who are you?"

"I'm Desmond, ma'am," I responded then turned to Grace. "Why did he do this to you and where is he at right now?"

"I don't know, but he did it because he claimed you called me Desmond. Is it true? Did you call me earlier?" Grace asked.

"Oh my God!" I replied as my phone starting ringing. I knew that it was nobody but Lexi calling me.

The timing of all of this was just so fucked up.

"Grace, you and Desmond gon' have to play catch up later. You need to get checked out," the lady that was with her spoke up.

I was standing there at a loss for words. The sorry ass nigga had put his hands on her because I had called her. I felt disgusted and enraged. All of the feelings that I had for Grace came rushing through me and seeing her like that broke my soul as I watched her and the lady that she was with walk off and check into the emergency department.

Feeling torn, not knowing if I should stay with Grace or head to Lexi, my thoughts were interrupted with my phone going off again. Checking to see who it was, I wasn't surprised to see that it was Lexi calling me again.

"I'm on my way. I told you that I was in the emergency department!" I huffed annoyed.

"Well, you need to hurry up."

"Is everything okay?"

"No Desmond, I'm in labor! I need you here now!"

"Okay man, chill. You stressing you and the baby out all for nothing. I will be there in a few minutes."

Hanging up with Lexi, I went back into the emergency room waiting room to see if Grace and the lady was still in there waiting. Seeing that they were nowhere in sight, I turned around and headed for my car. Thankfully, I was parked close to the door. Doing a light jog to my whip, I jumped in then headed to the other side of the hospital where the labor and delivery department was located.

Lexi said that she was in labor, but I figured I should wait until I saw for sure that she was indeed about to have the baby before calling my dad. Heading inside, I braced myself to deal with all of the drama that

I knew Lexi was going to bring. I should have been excited that my son was possibly about to make his entrance into the world, but at the same time, I couldn't shake the little encounter that Grace and I just had. Just the thought of that dude, whoever the fuck he was, putting his hands on her because I had called her phone had me feeling really fucked up.

# Chapter 6

### Grace

As soon as Malik left, I locked my front door then grabbed my cellphone. I was so scared and shook by what had just happened that I knew I was in no condition to drive myself to the hospital. I just knew that I didn't want Malik to take me, so I was thankful that he had finally left. I couldn't get him to leave fast enough. From the way I was feeling and the cut on my head bleeding out like it was, I knew I needed to head to the hospital as soon as possible. I didn't want to bring any attention to myself, so I didn't want to call 911 and request an ambulance, so the next best option was to call Kim.

"Hey girly, what's going on?"

"Are you busy?"

"I was just talking to Andre. Hold up so I can get him off the line."

As Kim clicked over to clear her line, my emotions were getting the best of me. I felt so foolish for putting myself in this position again with Malik. I was feeling embarrassed for having to call Kim and involving her, but I had no one else to turn to.

"Hey girl, what's going on Grace?"

"I need a very big favor." I cried, I was in pain and was feeling very shamed.

"Oh my God! What's up?"

"I really hate to ask you this, but can you please come take me to the hospital?"

"The HOSPITAL?! Okay, let me grab my keys." Kim said then continued. "What happened, Grace?"

"Me and Malik got into another fight. This time was worse than last time."

"That motherfuckin' bastard!" Kim snapped. "I'm on my way. Is his ass still there?"

"No, he left."

"Well, stay by your phone until I get there in case he comes back. If his ass shows his fuckin' face, don't answer the door call 911."

"I don't think he is planning to come back until later."

"What happened this time Grace? Earlier you two were all lovey-dovey. I don't understand what made him snap!"

"He claims my ex Desmond called my phone."

"He sure does have a lot of fuckin' nerve! All the bullshit with Chantel and he snapping over a dude calling you! I'm not trying to tell you what to do, but you need to leave his ass alone Grace!" Kim ranted.

I could tell that she was very upset.

"I know Kim. Trust me, I'm feeling the same way. Hell, I didn't even know my ex had my number."

"Wow! So, what if your ex did call your phone! That doesn't give that asshole the right to put his hands on you! I should be pulling up in less than five minutes. My ass doing damn near 80 miles per hour to get you."

"You need to slow down before you get pulled over and get a ticket." I chuckled. "You don't have to speed to get to me."

"Girl, this shit is an emergency. From the way you sound, I almost feel like hanging up and calling 911. Shit they will get to you much sooner."

"I thought about that before calling you, but I didn't want all that attention to my place like that. It's bad enough that one of my neighbors heard us fighting and came to my door to see what was going on."

"Oh wow! It was that bad?!"

"Yeah, it was pretty bad this time. He completely caught me off guard and snapped out on me."

"Damn Grace. Wow! I'm so pissed that he would do that to you. What an ass!"

I stayed on the phone giving Kim details of me and Malik's fight as I waited for her to get to my house. I truly believe had it not been for my next- door neighbor, Malik probably wouldn't have left when he did. When Kim told me that she was outside, I grabbed my purse and keys, locked my front door then headed to her car.

As embarrassed as I was, I was more hurt. When Kim saw me walking all slow, she jumped out her car and ran over to help me. With the pain that I was feeling, I was more concerned about getting to the hospital than concerned with how I was looking. I did my best to clean the wounds that I had gotten from Malik, but I knew that my face looked battered and bruised.

I decided to put on a PINK jogging suit to cover my legs and arms because they were just as battered and bruised as my face. Thankfully, it was evening time and the sun had gone down. I didn't want any of my neighbors to be able to look out of their windows and see how badly I looked.

Once we made it to Kim's car, I couldn't hide my face. As soon as I she was back in the driver's seat, light in her car turned on. I felt like a damn spotlight showcasing my face.

"Oh My! Fuck! Ah Heeeeelllllll nah Grace!!" Kim bellowed turning in her seat as I struggled to get comfortable in her car. Every single part of my body ached.

"Grace! What the fuck!"

"I know. I look bad, I know."

"No, you look fucked up! That nigga done put his fuckin' hands on you for the last time! I'm sorry Grace," Kim ranted as she sped off heading to the hospital. "You need to leave that nigga alone before he kills you Grace! Oh my God!" Kim cried as she reached one of her hands out to hold one of mine.

"I can't believe he did this to me."

"Shit, I can't believe it either. I really was trying to give dude the benefit of the doubt, but no Grace. You gotta leave him alone. He has to pay for this shit!" Kim continued to rant.

I couldn't even be mad at her for all that she was saying because it was the truth. I couldn't even say anything to defend him nor myself this time around. He was dead wrong, and I was just as wrong for letting him back into my life.

"You do plan on notifying the police right?"

"Uh, I think that will piss him off even more. That's the last thing I'm trying to do."

"Girl FUCK him!!!! Who gives a fuck about him getting pissed?! He needs to be held accountable for what he did to you Grace."

As Kim continued to drive to the hospital, my phone started vibrating in my purse. Taking it out, I saw that it was Sabrina. I knew that I couldn't answer her call because the last thing I wanted to do was worry her. I let the phone ring until my voicemail picked up.

"Was that him?" Kim asked as she glanced over at me.

"No, that was my stepmom."

"Why you ain't answer?"

"I'll call her back."

"She doesn't know, does she?" Kim asked.

"Nope and I want to keep it that way. She is all the way in Vegas, so the last thing I need is for her to be out there stressing about what's going on with me."

"She probably already worries about you Grace. You really need to let your family know what is going on just in case."

"In case of what?"

"In case that nigga take the shit too far next time and something really bad happens to you."

"There won't be a next. I can promise that," I assured her.

"I sure hope you're serious about that."

I sat there silent as I did my best to tune out all that Kim was saying. Not because she was saying anything wrong. Everything she was ranting about Malik was the truth. I was just tired of hearing it. None of what she was saying was going to change anything that happened tonight. Plus, it was making me feel worse than I already was feeling.

"Okay sweetie, ready? Let's go get you checked out," Kim said as she parked in the emergency parking section at the hospital.

Not answering, I sighed as I took a deep breath before exhaling, trying to brace myself for what was to come. I was so embarrassed and not sure how I was going to handle all of the questions that were about to be asked. I opened the car door then let Kim help me to the emergency room entrance. The closer we got to the entrance, I noticed that someone was standing at the door. When I took a closer look, I almost shitted. The person standing at the door was Desmond. What an unexpected coincidence!

I did my best to walk pass him as he held the door open for me and Kim. I prayed that he wouldn't notice me, but as my luck would have it, he did.

"Grace!" I heard Desmond say as I did my best to walk pass him with my head held down. "Oh my God! Grace what happened to you?" he continued as I tried to keep walking.

When I didn't answer, he continued to call out to me. Kim, realizing that Desmond knew me but ignoring the fact that I was trying to ignore him, decided it was her place to speak for me.

"Her crazy ass fuckin' no good ass boyfriend put his dick beaters on her!" she snapped and if I wasn't already embarrassed, I was definitely feeling shame at that point.

Desmond was just as shocked as I was by what Kim had said.

"Excuse me ma'am, but what did you say? Did you say her boyfriend did this to her?"

"Sorry Grace but I'ma tell it," Kim responded then continued. "Who are you?"

"I'm Desmond, ma'am," he responded as he looked at me. I couldn't even look at him. I was so embarrassed. "Why did he do this to you Grace? Where is he at right now?" Desmond asked as he looked around.

"He did it because he claimed you called me Desmond. Is it true? Did you call me earlier?" I asked. I needed to know if Malik was lying to me about Desmond calling.

"Oh my God!" he replied as his phone starting ringing.

I could tell by the look on his face that he did in fact call me. He had a look of guilt and anger on his face. Before either one of us could say anything else, Kim interjected.

"Grace, you and Desmond gon' have to play catch up later. You need to get checked out." The look that Desmond was giving me had me feeling some type of way. It was bad enough that I was already emotional, now I was beyond myself. Turning to walk away, I headed to the front desk to check in.

Once I checked in, Kim and I sat down in the waiting area to wait for me to get called to the back.

"I really wished you wouldn't have said anything to him."

"You can't be serious Grace. It wasn't like I told him anything he couldn't figure out on his own. Hell, you look like you been in a fight with Mayweather."

"Really Kim!"

"Seriously Grace, there is no denying that you took some blows tonight. Maybe I was wrong for telling him all of your business, but I'm pissed off that Malik's sorry ass did this shit to you."

"He wasn't lying to me. Malik said that Desmond had called me. I didn't even know that he had my number. I didn't even get a chance to see what he had called me for."

"Well, once you're ready, call him and find out. If he did call you his number should be in your phone," Kim said and with everything that had been going on, I hadn't even thought to check my phone call log to see if his number was in it. "From the looks of things, you'll be hearing from him soon. He looked pretty devastated to say the least and I don't blame him."

As Kim continued to rant, I started to replay all the events that had taken place tonight. Taking my phone out of my pocket, I went to the call log to check to see if Desmond's number was there. Knowing Malik, he probably deleted it or maybe not considering how he snapped out so quickly. I wondered if he even had time or thought to delete the number. Just when I opened my call log, I didn't think my night could get any worse. Hearing my name being called, I instantly thought... this couldn't be.

"Grace Lynn Jones!" the nurse called out again as my adrenaline started to kick in. Turning toward the voice calling my name, I wanted to pass out when my suspicions were confirmed.

Standing there frozen, unable to move, I locked eyes with the nurse, and she locked eyes with me.

"Grace, girl! Come on! Why you just standing there like that? What's wrong, why are you looking at her like that?" Kim asked as she attempted to get me to walk toward the nurse while questioning my behavior.

"That nurse is my mom."

# Chapter 7

## Malik

"Oh hey! What are you doing here?" Lauren asked as she opened her front door.

"What do you mean? Didn't you text and invite me over?"

I didn't know why she was acing all surprised to see me when she had texted me talking about she wanted to hook up and shit. She was standing in her doorway like she wasn't about to let me in.

"I did, but you said you were busy. I figured you were still busy so..."

"So, you gon' let me in or what?"

"Well, you kinda came at a bad time Malik," Lauren responded.

"A bad time?! What's going on Lauren?"

No sooner than I said that, I caught a glimpse of what looked like a man walking toward the front door.

"I have company over Malik. How 'bout I call you a lil later."

"I know you playin' right?"

"Well, not exactly."

"Everything good shorty?" Dude that she had up in her shit asked as he approached the front door.

"Uh, yeah Mike. Everything is fine," Lauren responded as dude stood next to her looking me up and down.

"Who dude?" I asked, feeling some type of way wondering why she would text me wanting to hook up if she had company already. I wasn't into that three-way type of shit, especially not two dudes to one chick. I didn't know what Lauren was on, but she had me feeling some type of way.

"He's a friend of mine."

"If you had company over, why would you text me asking if I wanted to hook up Lauren?"

"When you said you were busy, I figured we could hook up another time. When I didn't hear back from you, I made other plans. I told you that I had other male companions."

"Wow! Other plans huh?! Other male companions huh?"

"How 'bout I call you later or tomorrow-"

Standing there looking at her while dude stood next to her, I had to check myself. I wanted to reach out and grab both of their heads and bash them together. The fuckin' nerve!

"Alright, bet Lauren. I see what you on."

"Don't be like that Malik. I'll call you," Lauren replied closing the door in my face.

I couldn't believe she just shut the door in my face like that! She was lucky I wasn't in the mood to flash out on her ass. Hell, having to beat Grace's ass today was more than enough ass thrashing for me in one night.

Feeling some type of way, I headed back to my truck. Getting in the driver's seat, I decided to sit there for a while just to see if she would send dude on his way and call me. I knew that she wasn't trying to be in a relationship and had other dudes she fucked with, but the shit hit different having to see the shit so up close and personal. As much as she'd been hitting my line, I figured knowing that I had come by to hook up, she would get rid of dude and hit my line.

An hour later, her porch light came on then her front door opened. Seeing dude walk up out of her shit with an extra pep in his step damn near sent me into hysterics. Instantly seeing red just thinking about the shit she was probably in there doing to ol' boy had my mental fucked up. That and the fact that he was in there forever, I was ready to tear some shit up!

Jumping out my whip, I headed straight in dude's direction.

"Aye dude! Lemme holla at you right quick!" I snapped startling dude.

"Yo man! The fuck is your problem?!"

"You motherfucker! You disrespectful as fuck! Yo ass shoulda been left out my lady's crib!"

"Yo lady!" dude responded as he busted up laughing in my face.

"Ain't shit funny motherfucker!" I howled.

"Last time I checked, MY lady sent yo ass on then sucked and rode my big black dick!" Dude continued to laugh as I approached him. "If you know what's good for you, you'd take yo ass on bro!"

"I ain't yo bro, nigga!" I bellowed as I took a swing at dude's face.

I was beyond pissed off. First Grace had that nigga Desmond calling her line, now Lauren had some fuck nigga up in her shit getting rodded out all in my face. These women nowadays were disrespectful as fuck!

Before my punch could land on dude's face, he charged me taking me out by my legs. We both were putting in work going blow for blow. Even though I was on my back, I was still giving him a run for his money. Seconds later, I heard Lauren yelling for us to stop, but neither one of us listened.

"STOP IT!" Lauren continued to yell, but he continued to ignore her.

Although I was holding my own, I would be lying if I said that dude wasn't getting the best of me. He landed quite a few hard blows to my face and ribs. The more he punched my ribcage, the harder it became for me to defend myself. He stood up and delivered a hard kick to my side, knocking the wind out of me along with a few more blows to my face, busting my lip. All of a sudden, I heard a loud gunshot go off, causing dude to stop as I laid there trying to figure out through the pain that I was in, if I had gotten shot.

"Y'all gotta get from around here with all that shit!" Lauren yelled as dude stood over me looking at her like she was crazy.

Realizing I wasn't shot, but that Lauren had shot into the air to get us to stop fighting, I was thankful because dude was fuckin' me up, kinda like I had done Grace.

"This motherfucker stepped to me! Bet his ass know betta now!" Dude bellowed. "Get yo ass up and get the fuck on nigga before I fuck yo ass up again motherfucker."

"Y'all gotta go before one of my neighbors call the police. That's the last thing I need!" Lauren ranted as she held dude back. He was still trying to come for me as I tried to get up off the ground. "That's enough Mike!

He's had enough! If you don't stop, you gon' kill him!" Lauren continued.

"I don't hear you talkin' all that shit now buddy!" Mike continued to talk his shit as I got up feeling like he had cracked one of my ribs.

As I walked to my truck, Lauren and ol' boy went back inside of her house. I wasn't expecting dude to come at me like he did. He was lucky he caught me off guard. Otherwise, I would have fucked his ass up. It was cool though. When and if Lauren ever decided to hit me back, I was gonna make sure that her ass got hers for this bullshit going down like it did.

# Chapter 8

### Desmond

Making it to Lexi's room, she was laying in the hospital bed hooked up to an IV and a monitor that was tracking the baby's heartbeat. All throughout the room, all you could hear was our son's heart beating. Lexi's mom was also in the room with her sitting in a chair next to the bed.

"Well, look what the cat drug in!" Lexi said as soon as I stepped into the room.

"When you said to meet you at the hospital, I assumed you meant the emergency room. Hey Mrs. Jackson, how you doing?" I asked, acknowledging Lexi's mom.

"Hey Desmond, I'm doing great! Lexi not so much. We went to the ER first and when they saw that she was in labor they brought her here," she responded.

"It took you forever to get here! When I called you, I told you to leave right away. Had you done that you would have known that I was here."

"Well, I'm here now so try to chill. How you feeling? You good?"

"Shit I feel like my coochie about to fall out my ass!" Lexi hissed as her mom chuckled.

"That's how labor feels baby. When I was in labor with you, I felt like I was going to die."

"Really mom! Not now please."

I could tell that Lexi was in pain.

"Have you seen the doctor yet?"

"Yeah, I'm dilated four centimeters. Ouuuuuu! Where the hell dude at with the damn epidural! I feel like my body being ripped apart!" Lexi cried out in pain.

I went over to her bedside and held one of her hands then started rubbing her back. I didn't know what to do to help soothe her pain. This was my first time seeing a woman in labor. When Grace had Faith, I wasn't in the room with her.

"He is on the way baby," Mrs. Jackson consoled Lexi as she held her other hand. "Just breathe through the pain baby."

"Well, he need to hurry the fuck up! I can't take this shit!" Lexi continued to cry out.

I wasn't trying to downplay the pain that Lexi was in, but she was notorious for being a little on the extra side.

"Do you want me to go check to see what the hold-up is?" I asked trying to be of some kind of help.

"Please 'cause I can't take this pain much longer."

Just as I was about to walk out of the room, a female doctor walked in.

"Hello Ms. Jackson, I'm Doctor Harris. I'm here to give you your epidural."

"Thank God cause I'm about to die if another contraction hits. Ahhhhh ssssss!" Lexi cried out in pain.

"Just breathe through it, sweetie," Doctor Harris said as she walked up to the bedside table and laid out the supplies to give Lexi her medication. "I'ma have to ask you both to leave while I give her the epidural. It should only take a few minutes. As soon as I'm done, I will have the nurse Jackie come get you guys."

The doctor said as the nurse that was with her went to help Lexi get into position.

"Okay baby, we will be just outside the room. As soon as the doctor is done, we'll be back," Lexi's mom said.

"Okay, go so I can get this epidural shit! I can't take much more of this pain. Jesus Christ! Never again! I had no clue this shit felt like this!" Lexi ranted. To prevent her from seeing me chuckle, I scurried out the room.

Taking my cellphone out of my pocket as I walked out of her room, I called my dad.

"Hey son, how is it going?"

"Hey pops, welp, she's definitely in labor. Did the food get there yet? How is Faith?"

"Yeah, the food been here. Faith is good. She ate damn near the whole pizza." My dad chuckled.

"That girl sure knows she can put some food away to be so little."

"Shit, who you telling?" My dad laughed. "I'ma go get her and we'll be on our way up there."

"You sure? I can call you when she gets close to delivering."

"I'm positive. I don't want to miss being there for you and for the birth of my grandson. I'll see you shortly son."

"Thanks pops. We're in the labor and delivery part of the hospital. Her room number is 4243. See y'all when you get here."

Hanging up with my dad, I felt better knowing that he and Faith would be here for support.

"Hey Mrs. Jackson, thanks so much for bringing Lexi up here. I appreciate you. I just called my dad. He's on his way up here with Faith," I told Lexi's mom turning toward her as she stood outside of Lexi's room.

"No thanks needed. That's my baby in there. I wouldn't want to be anywhere else. How have you all been? I have been keeping you and your family in my prayers," she said as she reached out and hugged me.

"We have been hanging in there as best as we could. Thanks for that. We need all the prayers we can get."

"How has Faith been holding up?"

"She is as good as can be. She is a strong girl. Do you need anything? Are you hungry? Do you want me to run and get you something to drink?" I asked, trying to change the subject.

Talking about my mom was starting to make me feel some type of way. I missed my mom more than anything. It hurt my soul that she would not be here for the birth of my son. Touching the charm that hung on the chain around my neck, I remembered my mom saying that she would always be with me. She was right, that charm brought me comfort.

Ever since she put it around my neck, I could feel her presence. That was why I never took it off. It was the last thing she did for me right before she died, and I vowed to her that I would never take it off.

"I would love an iced cold Pepsi if you don't mind," Mrs. Jackson spoke up, interrupting me from my thoughts

"Okay bet. I'll be right back."

Walking off, I thought about everything that had taken place. I was still very upset about seeing Grace in the condition she was in, yet excited that my son was coming. I was a ball of mixed emotions and needed my mom now more than ever. I couldn't wait until my dad made it to the hospital. I needed to have him and Faith there to help me keep it together.

I stopped and asked where the café was from one of the nurses at the nurse station, then headed in the direction the nurse told me to go in. As I got closer to the café, I saw signs for the ER department, so I decided to go there first to see if Grace was still there so that I could check on her.

Thankfully, the ER wasn't too far. I made it there and saw that she was no longer in the waiting area. Neither was the lady that was with her.

Walking up to the check-in desk, I asked the nurse if Grace was still there. She said that she was checked into the back, but that was the only thing she would tell me.

Heading back to the café, on my way there, I decided to send Grace a text to check in on her.

**Me: Hey it's Desmond. Just wanted to check on you. I hope that you're okay.**

I hoped that Grace would respond. Hopefully, she wasn't upset with me for calling her. Had I known that her boyfriend was going to jump on her like that, I wouldn't have called her. That shit had my head fucked all up.

Making it to the café, I grabbed two bottles of Pepsi, one for Mrs. Jackson and one for my dad, a bottle of apple juice for Faith and a Lipton Iced tea for myself. Then I grabbed a couple of bags of chips and a bag of Cheese Nips figuring that we all could snack on them while we waited for Lexi to deliver. Once I had done that, I headed back to Lexi's room and got ready to brace myself for the birth of our son.

# Chapter 9

### Grace

"Girl what!?" I heard Kim say as me and my mom locked eyes.

It had been over 10 years since I last seen my mom and the very last thing that I expected was to see her now, especially in the condition that I was in.

"Dear God! What happened to you Grace?" my mom asked as she walked up to me and took my hand. "Come, follow me this way." She led me to the triage area behind a set of double doors.

Kim followed us as well, thankfully, this time she didn't say anything. I think she was just at a loss of words just as I was. Kim didn't know anything about why my mom and I stopped talking. All she knew was that we didn't get along.

"Is it possible for you to wait in the waiting area? Once she is put into a room, I will come and get you," my mom said to Kim.

"Grace, are you okay with that?" Kim asked.

"You can stay Kim," I responded.

Kim was the only person that I had that truly had my back. The way that my mom was looking at me, if looks could kill I'd be ice cold right now. The air between us was tense and very uncomfortable considering the circumstances.

"Grace, I would like to talk to you in private?" my mom said as she started taking my vitals.

"I got into a fight mom."

"With who... the Hulk?"

"Is that important? Wouldn't you rather know how much pain I am in? Or what's hurting instead?"

Here it was 10 years later, and my mom didn't even attempt to give me any kind of motherly love. I just didn't get it.

"How long have you been back in town?" she asked.

"I moved back a few months ago."

"I see. So, what exactly happened tonight?"

"I already told you that I got into a fight mom."

"And I asked with who?"

"I feel like one of my ribs may be broken," I said as I winced in pain.

"I'll chart that so that you can get an x-ray," my mom responded with her lips tight. "I can't believe that my only child has moved back to town and this is how I am finding out."

I didn't respond because I didn't know what she expected. Like, did she think I would send her a memo or something after how she treated me the last time we saw each other. I just looked over to Kim who was sitting there looking every bit as uncomfortable as I felt.

"I have to document who did this to you."

"You can put an ex," I told her.

"Desmond?!"

"No."

"Is he black?" she asked.

"MOM! What does that have to do with anything?" I couldn't believe that she would ask me that.

"I was just asking. What did you do for this 'ex' to do this to you?"

"Are you serious right now? I'm your 'only daughter' that you haven't seen in over a decade and not once did you ask me if I was okay, give me hug, nothing!" I was trying my hardest to hold back my emotions, but she was upsetting me more than I already was. Before I knew it, tears were falling from my eyes. I didn't know why my mom hated me so much.

"Why are you crying? I should be the one feeling some type of way. It's a shame that I had to find out that my child was back home by way of her getting her ass beat by some thug."

"Thug?! Really?! I can't believe that after all this time you all you can do is talk down on me and make things about you. Can't you see that I have been through enough already?" I snapped as Kim reached for one of my hands and held it.

"With all due respect ma'am, Grace has gone through quite a bit tonight already. Can she be checked in so she can be seen by a doctor please? She has been severely beaten and the purpose of me bringing her here is to get checked out, not to get into with someone else, mom or not."

"Pardon me, who are you?" my mom asked with an attitude.

"I'm her best friend Kim."

"Well Kim, if I wanted your input, I would've asked for it."

"Wow!" Kim replied as I squeezed her hand signaling for her to just let it go.

"I'm not making anything about me Grace Lynn. I am your mother and you have been in town for some months and haven't thought once to reach out to me," my mom said as she rolled her eyes and smirked at Kim.

"If you cared so much about my whereabouts why haven't I heard from you?"

"I thought I knew where you were, which was supposed to be with your father."

"He passed away, so I moved back."

"Your father passed away?" my mom asked sounding concerned. I didn't reply.

"A phone call would have been nice," she said.

"Really?! Why would I call you when you threw me away like yesterday's trash when I needed you most?!"

"Really Grace Lynn! I gave you an out to make something of yourself. A baby would have just complicated things."

When my mom said that, Kim turned and looked at me with confusion on her face. She didn't know that I had a child. I told Kim that me and my mom didn't get along. I left the part out about having a kid.

"How can you say that? You don't know that. It wasn't your choice to make. What you did to me has affected me ever since."

"How ungrateful Grace Lynn! I had to sacrifice to make a way for you when I had you. Disobeying my parents to be with your father was the biggest mistake I ever made."

"So that's why you hate me so much. I'm your biggest mistake. Wow! No wonder my life is so fucked up. I never stood a chance having a mom like you."

"Oh, so now it's my fault that you went out a found a man that beats on you. Wow!"

"Is there another nurse that I can see?" I asked. I was done with this surprise family reunion.

"Excuse me?"

"I want to see another nurse. I did not come here to be chastised by you. When you sent me on that plane to be with my dad you gave that right up. Clearly, I need to be seen by a doctor, not sitting here arguing with you. You've made your point loud and clear. You didn't want anything to do with me 10 years ago, so match that energy now and get me a NEW FUCKIN" NURSE!" I screamed.

At that point, I was beyond done.

"Grace calm down sweetie. I'll go get someone. This is some unbelievable shit," Kim said. As she stood up, another nurse walked in before she could walk out.

"Is everything okay over here?" the other nurse asked.

"If you weren't badly bruised as is, I would slap the shit out of you for talking to me like that! I am still your mother Grace!" my mom said then turned to the nurse. "No, everything is not okay. You can finish triaging her!" My mom snapped then walked off with tears in her eyes.

I didn't know why she felt like crying when I was the one that should have been upset and crying. A whole decade later and she still treated me like shit. I just didn't understand it.

"Hello, I'm Nurse Debbie. Can I ask, what was that all about?"

"I'd rather not say. Can I finish getting checked in so that I can see a doctor please. I've been in a fight, my head is bleeding, my ribs are aching and I'm in pain from my head to toe. And can I get something for the pain please?" I snapped.

"Sure honey. Let me get you to a room and I'll check with the doctor to see what to give you."

I didn't mean to snap at Nurse Debbie, but at that point, I had had enough. The nurse finished taking my vitals then Kim and I followed her to a room where she asked me to pee in a cup and change into a hospital gown. Kim helped me change because by that time I was in more pain than I was before I had gotten there. Before the nurse left out of the room, she said that she would be back shortly with some pain meds. Kim helped me to the restroom so I could pee in the damn cup. Once we got back to the room, she was full of questions about me and my mom.

"Grace, what the hell was that all about back there with your mom? I knew that you and your mom didn't get along, but that was some toxic shit I just witnessed. What the hell was she talking about?"

"Me and my ex Desmond, the guy that you just told all of my business to when we got here had a baby together 10 years ago. I hid my pregnancy from my mom, but when I had my baby, she showed up and showed out at the hospital. Long story short, she forced me to give my child up for adoption then put me on a plane to live with my dad in Vegas... the same day I was discharged from the hospital."

Kim was sitting there with tears falling from her eyes. "I don't know what to say Grace." She got up and sat on the hospital bed next to me and held my hand. "I'm so very sorry that you had to go through that."

"Thank you, I am too."

"So, you gave your baby up?" Kim asked with a sad and concerned look on her face.

"I had no choice."

"Wow!"

Before either one of us could say anything else, the curtain to the room was pulled back. Thinking that it was the nurse bringing my pain medication or the doctor, I was surprised when my mom walked in. I guess she was ready for round two.

"You know what... I'ma just say this then I'm done. I don't know where I went wrong with you Grace Lynn. I really tried to be the best mother that I could to you. I just don't know why you turned out to be the way that you are."

"Possibly because all you did was try to control me while you talked to me like I was gum on the bottom of your shoe. I did everything you asked of me and you still threw me away. What's crazy is, whether you want to believe it or not, I'm just like you mom."

"You are nothing like me at all. You got all of this ignorant shit from your father."

"Oh, now that is just enough!" Kim said as she stood up.

"I need for you to mind your business. This is between me and my daughter."

"It's okay Kim." Me and my mother needed to hash this shit out once and for all. I wasn't the scared little 15- year old she turned her back on years ago. I was a grown ass woman and she was going to know it after I was done with her. "My father that you're bringing up is the same man that you chose to sleep with and make a baby with against your parents' wishes. How is that any different than what I did with Desmond? You are such a hypocrite! And you don't need to keep bringing my dad into this when he isn't here to defend himself. How dare you!"

"How dare you come up in here and disrespect me like this?"

"Me disrespect you? Are you being for real right now? Just keep my dad out of this! He has nothing to do with this shit! This is between me and you! You can say whatever you want about me but keep him out of it!"

"I wish I knew why you are the way that you are."

"Look in the mirror and there you'll get your answer. You have hated me all my life because of the mistakes you chose to make in your past. I didn't ask you to make me. Why didn't you give me up like you forced me to do with my child! Lord knows I would have been much better off somewhere else than with you!" I snapped.

My mom stood there with tears in her eyes. I thought for sure she was going to lash out at me again, but instead, she walked away.

As soon as she snatched the curtain to the room closed, I busted out in tears. I was shaking in anger and crying like a baby.

"Please don't cry Grace. Fuck her! You have me, and I promise I will always be there for you. You don't need to ever want or need her in her life again," Kim said as she consoled me.

She held me in her arms and rubbed my back while I cried.

"All I wanted was to get checked out and sent home. I didn't want none of this shit!"

"Let me push that button so the nurse can get her ass in here. I'll tell you what though, if your mom brings her ass up in here again, I might sock her one good time," Kim said as she pressed the call button for the nurse causing me to chuckle.

I was laughing, but not because it was funny. But because that was all I could do to keep from crying again.

"I'm sorry I didn't tell you about my baby. I just-"

"Hey, there is no need to explain. I understand. I can't imagine how hard that must have been for you to go through at such a young age."

I felt my phone vibrate in my sweater pocket, so I pulled it out to check it. Seeing that I got a text from a number I didn't recognize, I opened and read it.

**Unknown Number: Hey it's Desmond. Just wanted to check on you. I hope that you're okay.**

Before I could respond, the nurse walked in to give me my pain medication.

# Chapter 10

## Malik
## The Next Day

Waking up to my body aching had me pissed off to the max. After leaving Lauren's house last night, I was so angry and in pain that instead of hitting Grace up like I said that I would, I just went straight to the crib instead. I thought that it was very fucked up for Lauren to have a nigga up in her shit like that, especially after she hit me up first wanting to hook up.

After getting into it with dude at her crib, I planned on leaving her ass alone. I was gonna miss fuckin' on her good ass pussy, but the shit wasn't all that to be fighting motherfuckers over. It was way too many women in this world to be fighting over one pussy. It definitely was a bad look for me because I wasn't that nigga.

Heading to the bathroom to take a piss, I checked the mirror and saw that one of my eyes had a blood clot in it. I was dark skinned, so it was hard to tell if I had a black eye or not... thank God. But you could definitely tell that my eye was swollen. That shit was fucked up 'cause I wasn't the one to be walking around with marks and bruises on my face.

After using the bathroom, I washed my hands then headed into the kitchen to get some ibuprofen for the pain that I was in. My side was killing me. It felt like one of my ribs was broken or cracked because every time I went to take a breath a pain shot up my side. My head was banging too. It felt like someone was playing the bongos on top of it and my hands were swollen and hurt from hitting on Grace as well as from fighting with dude.

Making it to the kitchen, I took four ibuprofens with a glass of water then checked the fridge to see if I had anything quick and simple to eat. I was in a lot of pain and really didn't feel like cooking anything, but I was a little hungry and didn't want to get sick to my stomach taking medicine on an empty stomach. Checking the fridge and seeing that it was damn near empty, I went to sit on the couch in the family room off the kitchen while browsing through the Uber Eats app.

Since it was a little after 12 in the afternoon, I chose to order from Rosati's pizza. I ordered a deep-dish meat lovers pizza with a side of fried mushrooms then kicked my feet up and turned the TV on to chill while I waited for my food to get here.

As I sat watching the highlights of last night's NBA game between the Lakers and the Bulls, I figured I would give Grace a call to feel her out.

I knew I was probably the last person that she wanted to hear from. I just wanted to feel her out because I hadn't spoken to her since I left her house last night. Knowing that she had gone to the hospital, I figured she would have called me and gave me an update on what happened. I hated that I flashed out on her something serious like I did, but figured if the police hadn't come looking for me by now, more than likely she hadn't called them and she didn't report my ass when she went to the hospital. Seeing that I hadn't heard from her, I figured she just needed a little time to get out of her feelings.

Hell, if anyone should have been upset it should have been me. She had no business having that Desmond dude calling her phone. Then to lie to me and act like she didn't know he had her phone number was fucked up on her part.

Picking up my cellphone, I went to Grace's phone number and pressed call. As soon as the phone started ringing, it clicked, and I got a busy tone. Hanging up, I tried calling her a few more times and the same thing happened.

"Hmph, I just know this broad ain't have me blocked!" I said out loud to myself.

She really knew how to get a rise out of me, and I was getting really fed up with her shit. I planned to wait until after my pizza got here and I ate something to see if the pain in my side would go down. If it didn't, I was going to go to the hospital. If the pain did go away, I was going to make it a point to go by Grace's house to see what was up with her blocking me again. It was now obvious that she was in her feelings, which was crazy to me considering it was her fault for lying that caused us to get into a fight. We had been doing good, our relationship had just got back on track then she went and had a nigga calling her phone. The fuckin' nerve!

Checking my Uber Eats app, I saw that the delivery person was almost to my house, so I tried getting up from the couch. The pain in my side hurt so bad that it took me a little longer than normal to get up off the couch. By the time I made it to the front door, the delivery person had sent me a text saying that I could come out to their car to get my food.

I hated when those Uber drivers did that shit. If I paid to have my shit delivered and was expected to give a tip, the very least their lazy asses could do was bring my shit to the fuckin' door!

I texted the driver and said I paid to have my food delivered to my door and if they expected a tip that they should get out of their car and bring me my shit.

My level of frustration was at an all-time high because I was in a lot pain and those four pills weren't helping not one bit. A couple of minutes after sending the Uber driver that text, my doorbell rang.

"Hi sir, did you order a pizza?" a cute dark skinned yougin' asked. She was so pretty that I couldn't even be rude to her.

"Yes, thanks for bringing it to the door."

"It's no problem sir. Normally, for safety purposes we have the customers come to the cars to get their food."

"I understand. If I wasn't in pain, I would have done just that. Thanks again," I said as she handed me my food then turned to walk back to her car.

I couldn't help but to stand there and stare at the phat ass she had on her. Baby girl was built like a brickhouse, but I could tell she was too young for my liking. What a sexy young tender she was, I thought as I closed my door then headed back into the family room. I couldn't even have an attitude with her.

Since I brought a large pizza, it was on special to come with a 2-liter of soda. Thank God because I didn't want to have to walk into the kitchen then back into the family room. The more I moved the more my side hurt.

Making it to the family room, I opened the pizza box and ripped the bag of fried mushrooms open and dug in. I was hoping that once I ate, it would help the pills I took take effect.

While I was eating, my phone started ringing. Thinking it was Grace, I checked it, and saw that it was Lauren calling me.

"I know this bitch done lost her fuckin' mind," I said to myself as I contemplated answering her call.

Just out of curiosity and because I wanted to give her a piece of my mind, I went ahead and answered.

"Hello," I dryly answered with attitude in my tone.

"Hey Malik, I just wanted to call to see how you were doing. Last night was crazy huh? I never expected for things to happen the way that they did."

"Is that so?"

"Well yeah. I was really taken aback to be honest. What happened between you and Mike anyway?"

"Huh? What do you mean what happened?"

"How did the fight start?"

"Look Lauren, you strike me as a very smart and intelligent young lady. You know exactly what happened. What's crazy to me is that you're taken aback when I should be the one feeling some type of way."

"How so Malik? You showed up to my house unannounced and unexpected. If anyone should be feeling some type of way it should be me."

"WOW! You had a whole disrespectful ass nigga up in your shit. What I want to know is why the fuck did you hit my line saying you wanted to hook up if you were meeting up with dude?"

"First of all, yes, I did hit you up, but didn't you say that you were busy at the time?! Like, I totally was not expecting you to just pop up at my house like that. To be honest, the way I see it is that's all on you. I told you from the jump I wasn't looking to be in a relationship with you or anyone else for that matter, so you should have known to not just show up to my house like that. That was what was rude."

"Dude sure didn't make it seem like y'all wasn't an item. At the end of the day, I'm not that nigga to be fighting over no bitch. All you had to do was keep it real with me and let me know what was up with you and dude and I never would have even fucked with your loose ass."

"You have a lot of fucking nerve. All the name calling is uncalled for. The way I see it, that fight was all on you. Like I said, Mike is a friend of mine that I see from time to time, not that I owe you any type of explanation. Had you taken your ass on like I told you none of that would have happened."

"So, you trying to say that shit was my fault!? You know what? Fuck you Lauren! Stay the fuck off my line with yo messy ass. You ain't gotta worry about me EVER popping up to your shit ever again. Ya pussy ain't worth all that drama—"

CLICK!

Before I could finish saying what I had to say, that simple minded ass fool hung the phone up on my ass. She was lucky my ass was in pain, otherwise, I woulda hopped in my whip, went to her crib and kicked her fuckin' ass!

That shit just pissed me the fuck off. How dare Lauren make it seem like I was the reason the fight with me and that fool happened last night. She was lucky I hadn't pressed charges on both of their asses. Hell, I was practically ambushed. All I was trying to do was let dude know that shit was foul, but he took the shit to a whole 'nother level.

Going to Lauren's name in my phone log, I deleted her shit. I was done with her ass. There were plenty more women I could get with that had decent pussy, including Grace's. I'd be damn if I was gone go back and fuck with her ass again. She really had me fucked up.

After I finished eating all of the fried mushrooms and half of the pizza I ordered, I was feeling a little better. My side was still killing me, the pills I took helped to take the edge off a little so that I could move around the house a little better, but the shit still hurt like hell.

Figuring I should shower and change clothes in hopes that a nice hot shower would help to ease the pain, I did just that. Once I was done getting dressed, the pain was back full force... plus, I was exhausted. Figuring that I should probably go get myself checked out, I decided to go to the emergency room.

Making it to the emergency room, I walked into the check in area and it was a full house. There were people in there with crying babies and kids running around with snotty noses. The nurse that checked me in said that there would be a wait, so I decided to head to the vending area to grab something to drink so that I could take some more medicine. I needed something to take the edge off of the pain just until I was able to get seen by a doctor.

When I went into the vending machine area what turned me off was the lady that was getting something from one of the machines had two small children with her; both kids clearly sick with some type of cold because their eyes and noses were running. They both were toddlers and touching all over the machines. When one of them sneezed then wiped their noses with her hand and went to touch the vending machine with the sodas, I felt disgusted. Not wanting to snap out and have everyone looking at me crazy, I got the directions for the café and headed in that direction.

To say that I was irritated would be an understatement. I was livid at that point. Not only did I have to wait until God knew how long to be seen by a doctor, I now had to walk to the hospital café just to get something to drink, so that I could take some more ibuprofen.

Making it to the café, I noticed this dude looking at me all crazy. I was a strictly coochie nigga. I loved me some pussy. This dude was starting to make me feel some type of way because he had a deadlocked stare on me.

Turning in his direction, I saw that he looked familiar. I just couldn't put a name to his face.

"Can I help you with something bro?" I asked, hoping he would take his ass on.

"Matter of fact you can. Would you by chance know someone named Grace?" dude asked and that was when it dawned on me who he was.

"Grace is my lady. Who wants to know?" I said with conviction.

Before I could say or do anything, dude scooped me up by the waist and slammed me to the ground. Somehow, my body twisted in mid-air causing me to land on my stomach. Then dude jumped on my back and put me in a crowbar position. All I could think was that he must have been a wrestler or at least watched the shit because his ass didn't give me any warning, but he had me in a fucked up position so quick I barely knew what was going on.

Hollering out in pain because that was all I could do, dude held me in that position as I prayed that he wouldn't snap my neck. I didn't know what his fucking problem was, but I had barely said shit to him for him to put his hands on me like this.

As I hollered out in pain, the girl that worked in the café tried to break us up.

"Sir, if you don't let that man go, I'ma have to get security!"

"Go get security... matter fact, call the police. I want you to. This motherfucker likes to put his hands on women."

It dawned on me in that moment that the person that just Rock Lesnard my ass was Desmond.

"Get... your... fuckin'... hands off of me!" I struggled to say, but the move that dude had me in I could barely speak.

"What's wrong nigga? You can put your hands on a woman... try that shit with me motherfucker!"

"Sir, sir! I called security. Please let that man go!" the café lady said.

Desmond ended up releasing me and all I could do was lay there and try to catch my breath.

"Put yo hands on Grace again motherfucker and you gone have me to deal with me bitch!" Desmond yelled as he sent a swift hard kick to my side causing me to black out from the pain.

# Chapter 11

### Desmond

"Put yo hands on Grace again motherfucker and you gone have me to deal with me bitch!" I growled as I kicked that nigga as hard as I could in his side. "Next time I catch your ass it's gon' be worse. You betta be lucky I ain't trying to tear this motherfuckin' store up with yo ass!" I bellowed.

I wasn't even the fighting type, but seeing dude caused me to snap. Although Grace and I weren't together, she was still the mother of my child. I had love for her and was still in love with her. I always felt that she was my soulmate. When she was sent away, it took me a long time to get over her leaving. Since then, I had never found anyone to be with that could ever compare to or fill her shoes. So, coming out of my element and snapping out on dude was a given. When I saw what he did to her, I knew in my soul that when and if I ever saw him that it was going to be on sight.

Turning to walk out of the café, dude's bitch ass just laid there like the punk that he was. Looking around, everyone that was in there was looking at me with wide big eyes as I addressed the lady that worked there.

"I'm sorry about that ma'am," I said as I dusted my hands off then shook my shoulders in an attempt to shake off the pissed off mood seeing that dude's face had put me in. "He beat up a lady friend of mine pretty badly. He deserved it."

The lady just stood there as she looked at me then over to dude on the floor, who was now grimacing in pain. Giving me a head nod as opposed to saying anything to me, she waited until I was almost out of the cafe then ran over to help assist dude's sorry ass.

Security didn't show up. Well, at least not while I was there. But if they would have shown up, I was prepared to let them know what he had done to Grace and ready to accept whatever repercussions behind slamming his ass. It felt good putting his ass to the ground. He had a lot of nerve putting his hands on Grace like that. When I saw her last night, all battered and bruised, it fucked up my mental. Hell, it shattered my heart and broke my soul. Then to know it was because I had called her phone really had me feeling some type of way.

Even though I was now the proud parent to a beautiful baby boy, I couldn't help myself when I saw dude walk his ass up in the café without a care in the world. To be honest, it looked like somebody had fucked him up before me. But since he wanted to address me about "his lady", I gave him what he needed... an ol' school can of whoop ass!

I tried to snap his neck off his shoulders. With the combination of grief and anger from losing my mom and the pain that I felt just thinking about what Grace had gone through when he jumped on her, I put all that energy into the swift kick I gave his ass. I hoped that I broke every rib bone he had on that side of his body with that kick. I wanted that nigga to feel and remember that lightweight thrashing I gave him every time he went to take a breath, so that he would be reminded to keep his hands to himself.

I had gone down to the café to grab something to eat because I was starving and ended up not getting shit. Lexi gave birth at 2:17 this afternoon to a healthy, beautiful, strong, precious little boy. Our son weighted a perfect seven pounds five ounces. When Mrs. Jackson, my dad and Faith had left last night, Lexi was still in labor. The three returned around noon today, just in time for the birth. My dad and Faith stayed until the baby was cleaned off and they were able to see him, then my dad took Faith home so that they could get some rest.

Lexi's mom ended up leaving shortly after my dad left, leaving me, Lexi and our little one alone to bond with our baby. Before I left to come down to the café, Lexi had just finished feeding him. Then I burped and changed him before I rocked him to sleep. By the time I got him to sleep, Lexi had passed out and was snoring louder than a grizzly bear.

I figured she had to have been exhausted from giving birth to our son. Her labor started out a little on the ruff side, but once she got that shot in her back, she was good to go.

Making my way back to her room, I heard her in the room talking to someone. Opening the door, I saw that it was a representative from the hospital bringing the birth certificate paperwork along with some forms to complete if she wanted the baby to get hospital pictures done. The birth of my son was completely different than the birth of my daughter.

When Grace had Faith, I wasn't in the room. Then once her mom came and made us all leave, I wasn't able to bond with Faith like I was able to with my son. Thankfully, the adoption process for Faith didn't take very long, but the circumstances around her birth were so very different then what I was going through with my son.

Once the guy walked out of the room, Lexi turned to me to explain everything that I had missed from their conversation.

"So, we have to decide on a name so that I can fill his birth certificate paperwork out," Lexi said as she filled in the information on the birth certificate form.

"How about naming him Desmond junior?"

"No way, that's way too cliché. I could see if we were married, then I might consider that. I was thinking something more like Ace or Major."

"I'm really not feeling either one of those names."

"Why not? I personally think he looks like an Ace," Lexi rebutted and all I could do was shake my head.

That feisty attitude of hers had come back. So long to the pleasant down to earth person she was after right she had the baby.

"I don't want to argue with you over our son's name Lexi. Although, I would like to have some input, but if you want to name him Ace since you are his mom, then Ace it is," I replied, trying to keep the peace with her. I was still in my feelings from having to snatch Grace's boyfriend up. I didn't want to bring any of that energy into the room around Lexi nor my son. "Can he at least have my last name?" I tried to reason.

"Actually, I was thinking about that. At first, I was going to give him my last name, but I think he should have your last name since he is your kid also."

"Well, isn't that nice of you." I smirked then caught myself from saying anything else.

As bad as I wanted to snap on her ass, especially since my adrenaline was still pumping, I figured it was best for me to just go with the flow.

One thing that I hated to do was argue. I may have been a state champion wrestler since the 5th grade, but I still had a very laid- back personality. I was that kid that just sat with my headphones in my ear before my matches and zoned out. I wasn't like all those other kids that liked to jump around like Rocky Balboa before their matches. I was that kid that sat there, hit the mat, and when the whistle blew, I took my opponent down, most of the time in the first round.

So, being with and around Lexi who lived for confrontation was just a turn off for me. Most times, it caused for me to clam up and just give her her way to keep things from escalating. I wasn't about to sit there and argue with her about a name, even though it was the name for our son. She was the mom and felt she had the final say, so be it.

Had I fed into her charade, I would have flashed out on her and probably said some things I wouldn't be able to take back. So, if she wanted to name our son Ace, then Ace it was. As long as he had my last name, I was good. Now, his last name was something I would have put up a fight over.

I still hadn't told Lexi about Faith being my daughter. I figured that was something that I would share with her once the cat was officially let out of the bag and I had to opportunity to speak with Grace. The only people other than some of my close relatives that knew about Faith were us and I didn't feel that it was something to share with Lexi just yet.

Plus, I knew if I would have told her she would have found some way to turn it into a negative and possibly say something slick about it. That was just who Lexi was, she always had something slick to say about EVERYTHING.

"Your signature goes here," Lexi said, breaking me from my thoughts as she pointed to the line where I needed to sign on the birth certificate form.

Ace Dion Holloway was my son's name and I had to admit that I was feeling very proud to be his dad. Throughout Lexi's pregnancy, I was most concerned about bringing a child into the world with her, but now that he was here, none of those concerns mattered. I vowed to do whatever it took to keep the peace with his mom just on the strength of him. He didn't ask to be here, and he definitely didn't deserve to have his parents bickering and fighting.

"So, which poses do you like? I like these and this one. Oh, and these two here," Lexi said, showing me the baby poses offered on the photo form.

"Whichever poses you like, I'm cool with. Hell, how much would it be to get them all done?"

"I'm not sure. Let me add it up."

"You know what? It doesn't even matter. Just fill it out, pick the poses you want. If you want them all, that's fine and I'll complete the part for the payment."

One of the things that my dad told me that I fully understood was that sometimes just to keep the peace it was best to not disagree with women, unless it was something that I fully stood on.

After sitting with her and little Ace for a couple more hours, I couldn't ignore the hunger pains that were in my stomach. Not only that, I needed to shower and change my clothes. The hospital food that they brought to the room was decent, but I needed some real food.

"I'ma run to the crib to shower and change. I promised I would bring Faith back up here to see Ace, so she'll be coming back up here with me."

"So, you're not going to spend the night with me?"

"I didn't say that. My dad will take Faith back home with him when he comes up later. He was so proud. I could tell that they both have fallen in love with Ace already."

"I guess that's fine. My mom probably coming back up here also."

"Do you want me to bring you anything up here when I come back?"

"No, I'm good. I just need some rest. I'm so tired."

"I promise I won't take too long," I replied, giving her a kiss on her forehead. Then I walked over to the bassinet bed that Ace was sleeping in and rubbed his back.

"Please don't wake him. The moment he gets up he is going to want to eat and my breasts need a break."

"You might as well get used to it 'cause he is a growing boy and is going to need all the titty milk he can get." I chuckled, surprisingly Lexi giggled. "I'll see you in a few hours. Try to get some rest before he wakes back up. If you want, I can tell the nurse on my way out to come take him to the nursery."

"Oh no! My baby is staying in the room with me. The way Lifetime been playing those movies about people abducting babies, I would tear this damn place up if something like that happened to him."

"Really Lex, no one is going to take him."

"You don't know that to be facts. He is good right where he is at."

"Okay, well I'll be back in a few."

Leaving out of Lexi's room I pulled my phone out and figured I'd try to reach out to Grace.

# Chapter 12
## Grace

After leaving the hospital last night, my emotions were all over the place. Thankfully, Kim was with me because I would have lost it if I didn't have her support. Not only was I upset about Malik putting his hands on me but seeing my mom after all that time was so unexpected. Being the best friend that Kim was, she offered for me to spend the night at her house and I was more than happy to accept.

After Malik jumped on me, then left last night, he mentioned that he would be back over to my house. The very last thing that I wanted was to be bothered with his ass. Matter of fact, I was done with Malik, for good this time.

After getting into it with my mom, she finally left me alone, so that I could get checked out by a doctor. When the doctor told me that my ribs were badly bruised, I had a concussion from the head blows and falling and hitting my head on the ottoman. I had to get six stitches on the cut on the side of my head. The doctor told me that I would need to take some days to rest, which would affect me going to work. I knew that I could never ever give Malik the chance to get upset and jump on me again. As bad as he had beaten me this time, who was to say that the next time he wouldn't kill me.

The doctor tried to get me to tell him what happened and after much push back and convincing from Kim, I ended up reporting Malik. The police were called and everything. When they showed up to my room in the ER, they filed a report and took pictures of all of the injuries and bruises that I had sustained from Malik beating on me. Knowing that he would kill me once he found out I had gotten the police involved, I knew that I had to keep my distance from him.

Kim was so proud of me when meanwhile, my nerves were all over the place. Once we left the hospital, I went into my phone and blocked Malik's number. I didn't want him having any contact with me. I was embarrassed, hurt and disappointed not just in him but in myself as well. I should have never given him another chance like I did.

While I was in the ER, one of the nurses had talked to me about how important it was to take domestic violence seriously. When she started talking about all the statistics of women who weren't lucky enough to make it out of violent relationships, to say that I was scared was an understatement. I knew that I had no choice but to stick to my guns and leave Malik alone.

After what seemed like forever, I was finally given a prescription for some pain medication and discharged. Since it was very late at night, the nurse that was helping me gave me a dose of pain medicine before I left.

As Kim and I rode to her house in silence, all I could do was think about all the events that had happened. From the fight with Malik, to seeing Desmond and learning that he had actually called my phone and seeing my mom...it was all just too much. I had no idea how Desmond had even gotten my number or what it was that he needed to talk to me about. I had so much going through my mind that it was making my head hurt even more than the cut and concussion that I already had.

Making it to Kim's house, it was pretty late. Since I didn't have a change of clothes, she gave me a long t-shirt to sleep comfortably in. Finally, I got in bed. As soon as my head hit the pillow, I was out like a light.

The smell of bacon cooking woke me up from my sleep. I was in so much pain that I could barely move, but I needed to use the bathroom. I slowly got out of bed and headed to her spare bathroom in the hallway. Once I was done, I slowly walked down the stairs and headed for the kitchen.

"Oh, hey suga! What are you doing out of bed?" Kim asked when she noticed me struggling to take a seat at her kitchen table.

"You have it smelling so good up in here, I couldn't help myself. Plus, I needed to use the bathroom and I needed some pain medication... badly."

"You should have called out to me. You need to be in bed resting. Didn't you hear what the doctor said?" Kim fussed as she flipped over the bacon that was frying in the pan.

"I know, but I'm not trying to be a burden to you like that."

"Girl bye! If I felt like that, I wouldn't have invited you to come over last night. Look, I was thinking, maybe you should stay here for a few days. At least until your wounds heal..." Kim began but I cut her off.

"Oh no! I can't do that to you."

"Oh yes, you can. I insist actually. Especially with Malik's ass lurking. At least until you get word back from the police that his ass has been arrested. I wouldn't be able to live with myself if I took you back home and he was to pop up and jump on you again."

"Ugh! I guess I didn't think of that."

"Exactly, so I will go by your place in a little while and grab you some clothes and toiletries. Plan to stay here for a few days, weeks... whatever you need until you get better."

"Thank you so much Kim. Seriously, thank you for everything."

"No thanks needed suga. You're like a sister to me. There isn't anything that I wouldn't do for you Grace."

"Do you think that it's a good idea for you to go to my house alone?" I asked, thinking what if Malik was lurking by my place and confronted her.

"Well, I was actually going to talk to you about that. I wanted to ask you how do you feel about me taking Andre with me? I won't go into detail with him about what happened, but he and I are supposed to meet up for lunch and I figured Malik wouldn't dare pull anything if he were to pop up and Dre was there."

"I'm cool with that. I don't see anything wrong with that at all. You know Andre is cool peoples. Actually, it makes me feel better because I would hate for Malik to be there lurking and approach you."

"Girl bye! Let me show you something sweetie," Kim said taking the cooked bacon out of the frying pan then walking off.

Moments later, she came back into the kitchen and showed me this black and pink box looking device she was holding. Pressing a button on the thing in her hand, it lit up making a static sounding noise.

"Girl, see this?"

"What is that, crazy?" I asked, chuckling while holding my ribs because it hurt to laugh.

"It's a stun gun. Ain't nobody worried about Malik's punk ass." Kim laughed then continued, "I would light that motherfucker's ass up with this if he were to ever think about approaching me. Hell, I'ma go and get you one and show you how to use it for protection. If I would have known his ass was going to do you like that, I would have been gotten you one already."

"I swear your ass is crazy." I tried to laugh.

"Here, take one of these pills chile," Kim said, handing me two pills. "I ran out earlier and grabbed your prescription since Walgreens was closed when we left the hospital."

"Thanks so much. Lord knows I need this because the stuff they gave me last night done worn off."

"No thanks needed suga."

"How much was the prescription?" I asked.

"Not much, don't worry about it."

Taking the pain medicine with the glass of orange juice that Kim had given me, I dug into the food that she placed in front of me. She had cooked French toast, bacon and scrambled cheesy eggs.

"Don't forget to call the police department to check to see if they were able to arrest that fool's ass," Kim reminded me.

"I know. I will call them as soon as I finish eating. You know what scares me?"

"What's that suga?"

"He was adamant on me not calling the police on him. Once he finds out that I reported him, he is going to go off."

"Girl fuck him! His ass is going to jail!"

"That's easier said than done when I have to see him at work."

"Well, you don't have to worry about that. Like I said, they are going to arrest his ass. Hopefully, he doesn't make bond so he can sit there for a while. As far as work is concerned, I thought about that and figured for the next couple of weeks, I'll have you work from home. As for the office work like filing, copying and report binding, I'ma call in for a temp and have them take care of it. You know we have that big VP meeting this week and the reports need to be put together. Other than that, there really isn't anything major that I need for you that requires you to actually be in the office."

"Oh no, I can't have you do that. It's my responsibility, that's my job. That's what you hired me for."

"Like you just said, I hired you so I can make the decision to do whatever I please. You need to be home resting. Don't worry, while you're in bed you can work on the important stuff. All that other office shit a temp can do. Hell, Kraft is paying for it out of the budget they gave me to run my department. I could see if I was having to pay out of pocket for a temp. I ain't tripping, so neither should you boo."

"Thanks Kim, you're such a blessing to me," I replied, letting out a long sigh.

I felt so bad. Ever since I had gotten involved with Malik, I felt like I had become a burden to Kim when that wasn't what I ever wanted. I hated that my personal life was affecting the responsibilities of my job.

"I know you feel bad for me having to get another temp, but truly, it's not biggie. You are great at what you do Grace. What kind of friend would I be if I didn't look out for your safety?"

"I get that and truly appreciate you for it. It's not fair that my personal life is affecting my job though."

"Girl bye! It's all good. I promise you I ain't tripping. Plus, if you stay here for a while, you can look out for Maxi while I'm at the office. So, consider us even."

"Oh God, I swear you treat that dog like she's your kid."

"Shit she is." Kim laughed as she gave Maxi a piece of bacon.

"So, have you given any thought to what your ex could've wanted to talk to you about? What a coincidence running into him at the hospital last night, huh?"

"I know right. To be honest, I have no idea what he wanted. We haven't talked since..." I paused, thinking about the day I had to give my child up. Of course, we had spoken when I first got back in town, but that day always played in my memory when I thought of Desmond.

"It's okay. You don't have to think about all of that right now. I wasn't trying to upset you," Kim said apologetically.

I was sure she could tell from the look on my face how I was feeling.

"It's okay. Look, I'm sorry I hadn't told you about all of that before last night. You and I are too close for me to have kept that from you. It's not something that I ever talk about. Having to give up a child is something that I have struggled with ever since it happened."

"I understand suga. But just know, when and if you ever want to talk about it, I am here. I will say this then I will leave the subject alone. Baby... your mom is a piece of work!"

"I know, tell me about it." I chuckled, even though nothing about that was funny. "The way she treated me after she and my dad divorced still haunts me 'til this day. I really feel like she hates me. As bad as I wish that weren't the case because I could have really benefited from having a caring mom growing up, I have learned to accept it. When she made me give my daughter up and shipped me away, I knew then just how deep her hatred for me was. Last night caught me off guard, but at the same time, I'm really not surprised by how she reacted."

"Girl, I just can't imagine. But you don't ever have to feel unwanted or alone now that you're in my life. I will always be there for you. You're like the sister I always wanted and never had. Fuck her! You don't need all that negativity in your life anyway. It's just crazy to me. Moms like her you read about or see in movies."

"Well, for me it's a reality. When I had my daughter, I vowed to never treat her the way my mom treated me. I was so proud to have a daughter so that I could break the cycle, but I wasn't given the chance to raise her." I cried.

"Aww suga, don't cry. If you want, I can help you find your daughter."

"Her adoption was closed. You won't be able to find any information on her because I have tried."

"I'm so sorry suga."

"It's fine. I think I'm going to go lay down. This pain pill done kicked in."

"Okay, let me help you to the room. Then I'm going to go get dressed so that I can run to your house and get you some clothes. Text me anything specific that you want me to grab. I'll be sure to get it. I'll be gone for a little minute because Andre and I are going to have lunch. Will you be okay for a little while?"

"Yea, I'll be fine."

"Okay, don't forget to text me what you'd like me to bring for you," Kim said.

"Okay, sounds good."

"Are you sure that I'm not imposing?"

"I'm positive suga. Get you some rest and I will see you in a little while."


### Later that day…

My ringing cellphone woke me up from the deep sleep that I was in. The pain medicine that I took had me in rem sleep. Reaching for my phone, I prayed that it wasn't Kim and that something bad hadn't happened.

Seeing that it was an unfamiliar number, I decided to answer thinking that it was the police department getting back to me about Malik. Praying that it was the police telling me that they had arrested Malik's ass, I sat up and answered my phone.

"Hello."

"Hello, Grace... this is Desmond."

# Chapter 13

## Malik

When that fuck boy Desmond pulled that wrestling, MMA, UFC move or whatever the fuck that was on me, I was not ready at all. It was bad enough that I was already at the hospital to get checked out for the fight that I had gotten into last night. Then for Grace's ex to attack me for no reason the way that he did was really fucked up on his part. For all I knew, she had probably convinced him to do that shit. I wondered if that was why she had me blocked from being able to call her.

He had a lot of nerve for doing that. He was lucky I was already at a disadvantage, otherwise things would have gone much differently for him. When he kicked me in my side, I could have sworn that I heard my ribs crack. The pain was so bad that I blacked out for a few minutes.

I could have strangled the lady in the café for not calling the police or at least hospital security to help me out. Instead, she stood by and watched that nigga practically rip my head off my shoulders. After he had left, she came rushing over to me and tried to help me up. Since she couldn't help me get off the ground, and I was clearly in too much pain to get up off the ground myself, she called the emergency department for them to send someone to help me out.

"Oh my God, sir! Just stay there, try not to move. Help will be here shortly," she said nervously as I laid on the ground feeling like a fool. I was more than sure that I looked like a damn fool too.

I couldn't even talk because the pain was so bad. All I could do was lay there in pain, moaning and groaning.

A couple of minutes later, some male nurses, patient porters or whoever they were showed up and helped me off the floor and into a wheelchair. I was hurting so badly that I couldn't do anything but grimace as tears fell from my eyes.

I didn't care if I looked like a punk or not. I had never felt pain like I was feeling ever before, so it was what it was.

The dudes wheeled me to the emergency department and thankfully, I was taken straight to the back, so that I could be seen by a doctor right away. I was so thankful because Lord only knew I did not want to have to sit and wait in the waiting area with all of those crying babies and kids with runny noses running all around.

Shortly after I was taken into a room, a nurse came in and took my vitals. Then she helped me into a hospital gown.

"Is it really necessary for me to put this gown on? I think it's too small. Shit, my whole backside is out."

"Yes sir, it is, and one size fits all. I'm sure the doctor is going to want to order X-rays, so you need to change into it," the nurse said as she helped me take my shirt off.

Not wanting to put up much of a fight, I was thankful that she was there to help me. If I would have been left alone to change, I didn't think I would have been able to do it myself. I could barely lift my arm on the right side.

"Can I get something for the pain? My body feels like it is on fucking fire."

"Yes, as soon as I put your IV in, the doctor will order something for the pain."

"IV?! There is nothing wrong with my mouth. Can you just give me a pill or something? Why do I have to get an IV?"

"It's just hospital protocol sir. Trust me, the IV meds are much stronger and way better than any pain pill. Considering the amount of pain that you are in, you will thank me later."

"I'm not really big on needles."

"Most people aren't, but you will be just fine. I'm one of the best at putting IV's, so you have nothing to worry about. Today is your lucky day."

"Ha, it sure doesn't feel like much of a lucky day to me," I huffed, not really feeling the whole idea of getting an IV.

The nurse helped me into the hospital bed, then pulled the bedside table over and laid out the supplies she needed to start my IV.

"So, tell me what brings you here today?"

"I fell down the stairs this morning and hurt my side," I lied. There was no chance in hell I was going to tell that nurse I got my ass tackled last night and just now.

"So, what exactly happened over in the café today?" the nurse asked as she prepped my hand for the IV.

I was so nervous about getting poked that I couldn't answer. I was sure that when the lady from the café called the ER to get me some help, she also told them what happened. I couldn't understand why the nurse would ask me such a stupid question. I was embarrassed enough, so I wasn't about to get into all of that.

"Okay, just try to relax your hand and breathe. You'll feel a little stick... that's the worst part."

"OUCH! Shit!" I bellowed. "Little stick my ass!"

"The worst part is over. The IV is in. I'm all done."

"Whew, so can I get something for the pain now?"

"So, what happened in the café?"

"I got attacked by a lunatic."

"Do you know who the person is? Would like to file a report?"

"I have no idea who he was and no... I'm good. I don't need to file a report. What happened is done and over with."

I didn't want to give her too much information because if I told her why Desmond and I got into it she would more than likely pry for more details. And I didn't want to have to mention anything about Grace being the cause behind it all.

"Wow! Well, I'm sorry that happened to you. I'm going to go get you something for the pain and the doctor should be in shortly."

As soon as she walked out of the room, another lady came in pushing a laptop on a cart. She took my demographic information so that I could get registered then took a copy of my driver's license and health insurance card. Ten minutes later, the nurse came back in and gave me something for the pain through my IV.

She wasn't lying when she said that IV meds worked better than pills.

As soon as I felt the medication go into my veins, it immediately started working. I was feeling so good that I forgot the name of the pain medication she gave me. When she left out of the room, I laid back on the bed, closed my eyes and waited for the doctor to come.

"Hello Mr. Wallace, I'm Doctor Bloomberg the attending physician on call today. I understand that you fell down a flight of stairs then got into a little bit of a scuffle a little while ago and you're having ride side pain."

"Yes, that is correct."

"On a scale from 1 to 10 where would you rate your pain level?"

"Right now, I'd say it's a two or three. Before the pain medication, I'd say about 1000."

The doctor did an exam on me and suspected that my ribs were broken so he put in an order for me to get an x-ray. Once the x-ray results came back, they confirmed that I did in fact have a couple of fractured ribs.

Finding out that getting into a fight with that thug at Lauren's house, then another fight with Grace's "ex" resulted in me having broken ribs really fucked up my day. If it weren't for the fact that I had broken ribs, I would have gone over to Lauren and Grace's house and broken every rib in their bodies.

Just when I thought that my day couldn't get any worse, it took a turn that I never saw coming. As I waited on the ER doctor to discharge me and give me some prescriptions for pain, the doctor walked into the room with three police officers in tow.

"What is going on? I told that nurse that I didn't want to file a report about what happened at the café."

"Mr. Wallace, we are not here for you to file a report," one of the officers that looked like the Rock from WWE said.

"Well, then what are you here for?"

"We're here because you are being placed under arrest."

"I'm under arrest?! Arrested for what? That lunatic attacked me! Just ask the lady in the café. She will tell you that I was there minding my business and dude stepped to me."

"I don't know what you're talking about Mr. Wallace. You are being arrested on an assault and battery charge that has been filed against you."

"Assault and battery! What are you talking about? I didn't assault or batter anyone!"

"You have the right to remain silent. Anything you say–"

"Wait a minute! Who did I supposedly assault?" I ranted, interrupting the officer from reading me my Miranda rights.

He finished rattling off my rights to me, then one of the other police officers spoke up.

"You are under arrest for the assault and battery against your girlfriend Grace."

"WHAT! What are you talking about?!" I bellowed, attempting to snatch my hands away from the police officer that was trying to put me in handcuffs.

"I need you to calm down, so we won't have to cause a scene. Any questions you may have can be answered down at the station."

At that point, I was done. The last thing I needed was to get manhandled by big ass husky police officers when I already had broken ribs. So, I complied and went with them without putting up a fight.

# Chapter 13

### Desmond

"Hey Desmond, how did you get my number?"

"It's actually a very long story. How are you? I have been worried about you ever since I saw you at the hospital."

"I'm okay, considering the circumstances."

"Look, I want to truly apologize to you if my phone call to you was the reason behind your boyfriend-"

"Ex-boyfriend," Grace cut me off and said.

"I'm sorry if I was the cause of what happened between the two of you."

"You calling definitely upset him, but it didn't give him the right to do what he did. You have no reason to be sorry."

"Look, I was hoping that we could meet up to talk. There is something that I need to talk to you about and it is best that we do it in person. I know that you may not be feeling up to going anywhere, and if you're not, I understand. How do you feel about coming by my parents' house?"

"What is this all about?"

"Like I said, it's better if we speak in person Grace."

"Umm, I don't know Desmond. I haven't seen your parents since... I don't know. I need to think about it."

"If it's because you feel uncomfortable coming by their house, we can meet somewhere else. I'm open to whatever you are comfortable with."

"When are you trying to meet up?" I asked, unsure of what this sudden urge to meet with me was about.

"As soon as possible."

"It sounds urgent, is everything okay? What does this have to do with? Are your parents okay?"

"I would say that it is urgent. My dad is doing good, considering. My mom passed away and we are still trying to adjust."

"Oh my God, Desmond! I'm so very sorry to hear that. Your mom was always so nice to me. She always treated me so good. I am so very sorry to hear that."

"Thanks Grace, I appreciate that. Actually, one of the last things she said she wanted me to do for her has to do with why I'm reaching out to you."

There was a long pause before either one of us said anything. I was praying that Grace would be open to seeing me so that we could talk.

"Well," she began to say, and the tone of her voice was unreadable. I had to brace myself for her to turn me down. "I can't come right now because I'm staying at my friend's house. I've been put on bedrest and my car is at my place."

"I understand. Would your friend be okay with me coming to see you at her place? I don't mind if you both are okay with it."

I wasn't trying to be pushy, but for the sake of my mom's final wishes and for Faith's sake, I really wanted to get this over and done with. Now with me having a son, I wasn't sure how Faith was feeling. When my mom said that there would come a time that Faith would need her mom, I truly felt that the time had come.

Faith was having to deal with a lot all at once. From finding out that I was her dad, to losing my mom and finding out that she had another mom that she had never met. Now, I had another child, so I could only imagine what she must be going through.

When Faith and my dad came up to the hospital the night Ace was born, she appeared to be very happy. But at the same time, the spark that she once had in her eyes was gone. If there were anytime that would be the right time for her to meet Grace, as long as Grace was open to it, I would think that time would be now.

"Ummm, let me give my friend a call to discuss this with her first. Can I call you back a little later?"

"Absolutely, I look forward to your phone call. I hate to be a bug, but the sooner I hear back from you the better. I have to go back up to the hospital today, but I will plan to do that around what you say."

"Is everything okay? I mean, you don't have to come today. You said you wanted to talk as soon as possible so-"

"I know I did. Everything is fine. My son was born last night. That was the reason why I was up at the hospital when I ran into you."

"Oh, congratulations on the birth of your son."

I could tell in Grace's tone that she was pretending to be happy for me. Now that I thought about it, I probably shouldn't had brought up my son. Although, she did see me and Lexi when Lexi was pregnant.

"Look Grace, I'm sorry about bringing that up."

"No, no, no sorry needed. I will call my friend now and get back to you soon. Thanks for reaching out Desmond."

Grace hung up before I could say anything else. Making it to my dad's house, I pulled into the driveway and parked my car. Sitting there for a minute, all I could do was think about all of the events that had taken place over the last 24 hours. Seeing Grace all battered and bruised, the birth of my son, kicking that jerk's ass for putting his hands on Grace and now, finally having a conversation with her after not speaking with her for over a decade.

Touching the charm on the chain that my mom gave me I said a prayer to her and God.

"Mom, I'm trying to do what you asked me to do without you here and I don't know if I can do this without you. I need for you and God to give me strength so that I can keep it together. Please let everything go the way that you would want it to go. I love you mom."

"Hey son, why the look of worry? You should be happy you're the proud dad of two very beautiful child," my dad said as I walked through the front door.

"Where's Faith?"

"She's up in the room with Bear. Why, what's up?"

"I just talked to Grace?"

"And? What happened?"

I told my dad how I called Grace, which led to her ex jumping on her and how I ran into her at the hospital. Then I caught him up on the phone call that I just had with her.

"Well son, you did your part. All you have to do now is just wait."

"I know. Waiting is always the hardest part for me."

"As it is for most people." My dad chuckled. "Have you eaten?"

"No not yet. I'm starving actually."

"Come, I grilled some chicken. I didn't make any side dishes to go with the chicken. You know side dishes was never my specialty."

My dad always grilled the meat and my mom was in charge of making all of the sides. Following my dad into the kitchen, I tore into the grilled chicken. My dad was what I considered a grill master. Anything he put on the grill came out tasty.

While I ate, I told him how I had gone down to the café to get something to eat but ended up kicking Grace's ex's ass. He thought that was hilarious but reminded me of the fact that I could have gotten arrested. He was right. I probably shouldn't have jumped on dude like that, but I couldn't help myself.

Even though Grace and I were no longer together, she was still my first true love and the mother of my daughter. There was no way that I wasn't going to handle dude on sight for what he had done to her. I still had lots of love for Grace, even after all of these years. I just hoped she didn't let me down and ghosted me.

After I ate, I took a shower and changed clothes. I hadn't heard back from Grace, so I figured I would go up to the hospital and sit with Lexi. Just as I was about to see if Faith wanted to tag along, my phone rang.

"Hey Desmond, it's Grace."

"Oh hey," I said, going back into my room and shutting the door.

I wasn't sure what she was going to say and if she didn't want to meet up, I didn't want to risk Faith hearing me say her name out loud.

"It's fine if you come by here. I can text you the address now. Are you still available to come today or-"

"I can get ready to come now," I said cutting her off. "Thanks so much for agreeing to meet with me Grace. I will see you soon."

Hanging up the phone, I went in search of my dad.

"Dad! Dad! Dad!"

"Boy, what the hell you doing all of that hoopin' and hollerin' for? Jesus Christ you bout gave me a heart attack!"

My dad was sitting in the den that was just outside of the bedroom that I was staying in.

"My bad pops. I didn't know you were down here."

"What's all the ruckus about?" my dad asked.

"Grace just called me back and she wants to meet."

"That's great! When are you guys meeting up?"

"Now."

"As in right now?"

"Well yeah! I figured the sooner the better."

"Okay, so do you want me to go with you?"

"I was thinking that I would meet up with her first and depending on how she feels about meeting Faith, maybe you can bring Faith to us."

"Where are y'all meeting at?"

"Her friend's house."

"Okay, is it far?"

"Not really. It's actually right by the hospital."

"Okay, how about I take Faith up to the hospital to visit Ace since we said that she could see him today while you chat with Grace. That way I can keep Lexi occupied so she won't be looking for you."

"Speaking of all of that, I noticed that Faith was excited about Ace, but at the same time she seemed a little sad."

"She and I talked about that earlier. Faith was feeling a little confused about Ace. She didn't know what he was to her. I explained that Ace is her little brother but that his mom doesn't know that you're Faith's dad just yet. This is all so new to all of us. It's going to take some time to make it all make sense to her you know."

"Yeah pops, I know. I appreciate you for having that talk with Faith. I plan on talking with her as well."

"When are planning on letting Lexi know?"

"I hate that I even have to tell her any of this, but I will let her know once I talk to Grace first. You know how Lexi is–"

"Oh boy do I know." My dad laughed because it was no secret that Lexi was over dramatic.

"I didn't want to tell Lexi because God only knows how she is going to take it. I wanted to see how things worked out with Grace and Faith first, then let Lexi know. I really don't feel like I owe her an explanation, but because she is the mother to my son, I figured she should know."

"I think that is a good plan because you are right. She should know, if not for her sake but for your kids' sake. Poor Faith wants to play the part of big sister so bad but knows she can't say anything just yet. I just feel like that is too big of a burden for her to be carrying."

"I agree with you pops. Well, if everything works in our favor, I'll be letting her know tonight."

"I would offer my support in being there for you for that conversation, but I don't want Faith there if Lexi starts acting out."

"I agree." I laughed.

It was a shame that Lexi couldn't see how her irrational behavior really made her look bad to people.

I headed out to Grace's friend's house as my dad got Faith so he could head up to the hospital to visit with Lexi and Ace. If Grace was open to meeting Faith, my dad was cool with bringing Faith over to Grace's friend's house.

As I drove to meet up with Grace, I would be lying if I said that I was not nervous as hell. I had no idea what Grace would say, or how she would feel about meeting with Faith. I just hoped that she would be open to it and that Faith meeting Grace was the right direction to go in.

Pulling up to Grace's friend's house, I was anxious to go inside. I had gotten so excited with everything that I realized that I hadn't called Lexi to let her know that I would be up to the hospital later than she originally expected. I figured since my dad was going up there, he would vouch for me since he knew what I was up to.

Just as I was about to knock on the front door, it opened and the chick that was with Grace last night at the hospital was standing there.

"Hey Desmond, come on in. Grace will be down shortly."

"Hello, uh–"

"Kim, my name is Kim, and this is my boyfriend Andre."

"Hello, nice to meet you," I said, shaking dude's hand.

"I appreciate you for reaching out to Grace and checking in on her," Kim began just as Grace walked up looking like an angel. "Oh, hey sweetie," Kim said to Grace as she walked up to us. "Dre and I will be upstairs. Let me know if you need anything. Desmond, make yourself at home."

There was a dog barking off in the background somewhere. Looking around, I didn't see it, so I figured it must have been locked in a cage or room.

"That's Kim's dog Maxi. She is upstairs acting the fool because she heard you knocking on the door. She'll stop barking once Kim goes to get her."

"Oh okay," I replied as I looked at Grace. She looked a lot better than she did last night. She still had bruises, but they weren't as profound as they were last night. "You're looking good."

"You don't have to lie." Grace chuckled.

"No seriously, you look a lot better today."

"You'd be surprised what a little makeup could do." Grace chuckled.

"How are you feeling though?"

"Considering everything, I'm okay. Congrats again on the little one. You must be so proud."

"Thank you... I appreciate that," I replied.

I followed her into the living room then took a seat across from her on the couch. There was a pause in our conversation because I didn't know how to begin to tell Grace about Faith. Figuring the best way to go about it was to just jump into it, but before I could begin, she broke the silence between us.

"So, what's so important that you want to talk to me about?" Grace asked, jumping right into it.

# Chapter 14

## Grace

"Well, first I want to tell you about something that happened earlier today before it is brought to you and taken out of context. I don't want anything to catch you off guard," Desmond said with a worried look on his face.

I had no clue what he was talking about. What exactly would he have to tell me that could be taken out of context if it got back to me?

"Okay. What is it about?"

"Your ex."

I almost choked when he brought up Malik.

"What about him?" I asked nervously.

"I ran into him today while I was up at the hospital. One thing led to another and things got physical between us."

"Physical how? How did you even know he was my ex?"

"When I saw dude at first, I wasn't sure if it was him or not. I thought he looked familiar from that day I saw you at the restaurant, so to be sure I asked him if he knew you. When he answered with a slick ass response, he confirmed it was him."

I wanted to puke. I literally felt sick to my stomach. The very last thing that I would have ever thought was that Desmond and Malik would get into a confrontation.

"I'm almost afraid to ask what happened. I have a feeling that things didn't go good."

"To be honest, I wasn't expecting him come at me like he did Grace. He got slick at the mouth and the next thing I knew I went for him and he ended up on the floor."

"Oh my God! Desmond!!"

Desmond used to wrestle back in the day, so I knew he was no joke when it came to fucking people up. Not only did he used to wrestle, but he was one of the best wrestlers in the state. I could only imagine what went gone down between the two of them.

"All I could think of was you and how he had jumped on you and all because I called you really had me feeling fucked up. I just wanted to let dude know that I wasn't trying to disrespect y'all's relationship by calling you the other night. But his fucked up response caused me to flash out. The next thing that I knew dude was on the floor. I should have minded my business, but it just wasn't sitting right with me what he did you."

"Desmond you really shouldn't have done that," I said as I looked at him like he was crazy.

He didn't have cuts or bruises, so I assumed that Malik got his ass handed to him. As shocked as I was, I had to admit that I was glad Malik got his ass kicked. He deserved that and then some for putting his hands on me.

I was still very taken aback by all of this. The fact that Desmond stuck up for me like that when he was in a relationship with another woman, who by the way, just had his baby had me speechless.

"I know Grace, and I'm sorry about that. You know, you will always hold a very special place in my heart Grace. You're the mother to our child, my firstborn. If someone fucks with you, they fuck with me too. The whole thought of dude putting his hands on you, I just couldn't let that go."

"I appreciate you for standing up for me, I really do. But really you shouldn't have done that because now I have to deal with him because of it. I'm sure he is probably stewing over this right now."

Worry started to set in and all I could think about was Malik and how he must be beyond pissed off with me. At the same time, I wondered what Malik was doing up at the hospital in the first place. I wondered was he there looking for me. I had him blocked on my phone, so

I didn't know if he had tried to reach out to me or not. I'm pretty sure that he did because I figured he would be concerned about what happened.

I blocked him because I knew that he was going to be very upset once he found out about me reporting his ass to the police. He knew before he left my house that he had physically hurt me pretty badly. That was the only explanation that I could think of for him to be up at the hospital.

I was also worried because I knew that at any minute, he was going to get picked up by the police for beating me up the way that he did. Now I was hearing that Desmond done kicked his ass too! Lawd have mercy, this was too much.

I tried to hide the fact that I was panicking because I knew for a fact that Malik was going to be out to kill me for sure now.

"I apologize again, but if you're concerned about dude coming at you, I doubt you will have to worry about him ever putting his hands on you again. I made it very clear to him what the consequences would be if he does."

"Oh my God, Desmond! I don't know what to say. You just don't know Malik like I know him though."

"Let's just say that I don't need to know him like you do to know you don't have to worry about him coming at you like that again. I showed his punk ass no mercy. He's lucky that we were in the hospital when that happened because if I would have run into him on the street somewhere, he really would have gotten his ass kicked. I just ruffed him up a little but trust me when I tell you, I got my point across."

"Oh my God!" Was all I could say.

"Not to get in your business more than I already have, but I hope you reported him to the law for what he did to you."

"I did. As a matter of fact, I'm waiting to hear back from the officer on the case. I pressed charges so I know once he is arrested, he is going to be pissed and now this too. I'd be lucky if he doesn't hunt me down and kill me. I really wish you wouldn't have done that."

"He is not going to kill you Grace. Is that why you are staying here at Kim's house?"

"Pretty much."

"Damn, I'm so sorry that you have to go through all of that. Like I said, you don't have anything to worry about. I promise you that."

There was a silence between us again. I didn't know what to say after all of that.

"Look, I know it has been a very long time since you and I were together, but I never stopped loving you

Grace. There isn't anything that I wouldn't do for you, no matter how much time has passed between us."

"I don't know what to say Desmond."

"Just promise me that you will stay away from that dude if he tries to come back around."

"You don't have to worry about that. Moving forward, I plan to make better choices with the people I date."

"I can understand that. I feel the same way," he said.

"What do you mean? You just had a baby. Are things not okay with you and your girlfriend?"

"Well for one, she's just my baby mama." He chuckled. "She and I aren't dating. I haven't had much luck in the love department since... well, since you actually."

I was taken aback by what he just said. Looking into his eyes, I could tell that he was being genuine. Desmond was my first and only true love and to hear him say that, I was that for him actually felt better than I thought it would have felt.

"I'm sorry, I just assumed that you were either married or still dating considering y'all just had a baby together."

"In a perfect world, that is how it's supposed to work. But we both know that this world is far from perfect."

"Yeah don't I know. Again, I'm sorry things didn't work out with you and your son's mother."

"It's nothing to be sorry about. It's a long story but the short version is we dated on and off and we just don't vibe. The last time we broke up was when I found out she was pregnant. Things were so jaded with us that I made her do a test to prove that the baby was mine. We got back together with the intent of starting a family, but we just can't get along. So, yes, we just had a son, but we are only co-parenting. We aren't dating. I can promise you that."

"Wow Desmond, that's too bad."

"Not necessarily. Hell, I was miserable with her."

I didn't know how to respond, so I figured I asked what was so important that he wanted to meet up with me to discuss. I knew it couldn't have been his fight with Malik because that just happened today.

"So, what did you want to talk to me about that was so important?"

After a long pause, he finally said something that I was not at all expecting.

"Do you ever wonder about our daughter Grace?"

"HUH? Excuse me?"

He had taken me off guard by that question.

"Do you ever think about our daughter?"

"Of course, I do. Do you?"

"All the time," he said.

"Is that what you wanted to discuss with me?"

I thought he had said earlier on the phone that one of his mom's last wishes was for him to pass along a message to me.

"Let me ask you a question. If you had the opportunity to see our daughter, would you be open to it?"

"Desmond, you said that you had a message to pass to me from your mom. Why are we discussing our daughter?"

"Because Grace, I want to know how you feel about our daughter before discussing anything else with you."

"I don't know where you're going with all of this, but if you must know, I think about her all the time. I even tried to find information on her adoption, but the adoption was a closed one, so I hit a brick wall. Most days, I try to accept things for what they are, but I'd be lying if I said that I don't wish they were different. Every day for the last 10 years I've thought about her. What about you? Do you think about her? Would you be open to seeing her if you could?"

"So, you're saying you would want to meet her then?" he asked, not answering my question.

"Desmond, what kind of game are you playing? Do you know who adopted our daughter or something? Is that why you are asking me all of these left field questions?"

"Well actually, yes."

"Pardon me?" I asked.

"Yes Grace. I know the family that adopted our daughter... very well actually."

"You do?! Well... who are they?"

"My family adopted her Grace."

"I'm sorry, what did you say?"

"When your mom forced you to give her up, I still had rights to our baby girl because I'm her dad. Since I was a minor at the time, my mom and dad adopted her."

"Oh my God!"

"One of the things my mom wished for right before she died was for me to find you so that you could get the opportunity to meet Faith and to be a part of her life."

"Faith? Is her name Faith?"

"Faith Lynn Holloway, actually."

"Oh my God!"

Getting up from the couch, I walked as fast as I could to the bathroom that was down the hall. I felt like

I was going to pass out. Hearing Desmond say that his family had adopted our daughter had taken me by surprise. I guess that was why he was trying to contact me.

Oh my God! Never in a million years did I ever think that I would see my daughter again and now here Desmond was, sitting in my face telling me this. All these years I had dreamed about the day I gave birth to her. I dreamed about the way she looked, how she smelled, the sound of her cries, which was the last thing I heard before she was taken out of my room. Some nights I would wake up in a cold sweat because I'd be dreaming about her crying... crying out for me just as I was crying out for her.

I didn't know what to think or what to do. All I could do was stand and look in the mirror as I silently cried. Then to find out that her name was Faith, and he and his family gave her my name for her middle name shifted something in my heart. My baby girl carried my name all these years and I didn't have a clue.

# Chapter 15

### Chantel

When Malik and Grace walked out of the office hand in hand on Friday, it confirmed that they were back together and on good terms. The sight of the two of them all happy and carefree made me sick to my stomach. I knew that I wouldn't have been able to continue to go to work with them every day and look at the two of them all happy and in love. Even though I didn't want to be with Malik anymore, the fact that I was just pregnant with his child then the loss of the baby left a soft spot in my heart for him.

I knew what I needed to do once they left. Logging back into my computer and opening up Microsoft Word, I opened a new document and typed two letters. One to Malik, and the other one to my boss.

The letter that I wrote to my boss was a letter of resignation. I had enough money in my savings to hold me over until I could find another job. I just couldn't do it anymore. I couldn't continue to work five days a week at a job with Malik and Grace. I knew to some people they might think I was crazy. Hell, Genie sure didn't hesitate to tell me how crazy I was when I told her that I was quitting, but I didn't care.

The way that Malik was hounding me to abort our child was just too much. Then to flaunt his floozy in my face like that was a special kind of disrespect. Since I planned on never seeing or talking to him ever again, I decided to let him know in a letter that I had miscarried our baby and wished him and Grace my best.

I couldn't tell him to his face that I had lost our child because I knew that I wouldn't have been able to handle how he would have reacted. Just thinking about how happy he would have been over something that was so devastating to me rocked me to my core.

After sitting my letter of resignation on my boss's desk along with my keys to the office, I placed the letter that I typed for Malik on his desk. Then, I packed up all of my belongings, logged out of the computer and left Kraft for the last time.

As I was leaving the building, I couldn't get out of there fast enough. As I was walking to my car, I ran into Genie and Erik in the parking garage. They both must have thought that I was already gone because they were cupcaking to death without a care in the world. I didn't even think that they saw me.

I loved Genie and I wanted nothing but the best for her, but I'd be lying if I said I wasn't jealous of her and Erik. They both wouldn't claim the other, but it was no big secret that they were messing around. Erik and Genie took a liking to each other from the moment Genie started at the company.

It used to be me and Malik and Genie and Erik going out to lunch together, all of us putting on and acting liking we weren't feeling each other. If I remember correctly, Malik and I started messing around before Genie and Erik. Genie and I had become very close friends both at work and outside of work, so we told each other everything.

Malik and Erik didn't know that me and Genie talked about all of us feeling one another. Seeing Genie and Erik all caked up bothered me a little because that should have been me and Malik had it not been for Grace.

I was throwing in the towel and giving up the fight for him. If Grace and Malik wanted one another they could have one another.

Over the weekend, I registered with a couple of online job finding sites and worked on my resume. With today being Sunday, I figured I'd take the day to run a couple of errands then to relax. Tomorrow, I'd get up and begin my official job search.

Leaving out the house, I headed to the nail salon to get a mani and pedi. On the way there, I decided to call Genie to see if she wanted to meet up for lunch.

Making it to the nail salon, Sarina took me right away. Sarina was the bomb. She was the only person I saw whenever I went to this particular salon. Since I always made it a point to tip her well, she never had a problem with taking me right away whenever I would walk in.

"Hey lady, how you want your nails done today? You want the usual?" Sarina asked, patting me on my shoulder.

She always greeted me the same way every time.

"I want the usual French on both."

Sitting in the massage chair and placing my feet in the pedi spa, I pulled my phone out of my purse to call Genie.

"Hey girl, what you up?"

"You just now getting up?" I asked because Genie answered the phone damn near sounding like a man. "Somebody must have had a rough night." I chuckled.

"Girl yasss! Erik been here since Friday and you know how that is."

"I don't know why y'all just don't make things official."

"Cause I ain't got time for people to be all up in our shit."

"Girl bye, it ain't like people don't know. I saw y'all all boo'ed up in the parking garage on Friday. Anybody could have walked up and seen y'all, so you must not care that much."

"Girl whatever. So, how does it feel not having to go into work tomorrow?"

"It feels good actually. I'm going to start my job search tomorrow. I'm sure it won't be hard finding another receptionist job."

"I just can't believe you up and quit like that. I don't think I could quit my job over a man and some chick."

"That's easier said than done. If you put yourself in my shoes and take into consideration everything I have just gone through, you'd understand why."

"I get where you're coming from. I just hate that we won't be working together anymore."

"I know but you acting like we don't kick it outside of work crazy. Which is why I'm calling you?"

"What's up?"

"Wanna meet up for lunch? I was thinking about Moondoggie's or Herms."

"Both of those sound good, but Erik still here girl. He's in the shower waiting on yours truly."

"Oh gawd! TMI friend."

"We can meet up tomorrow for lunch if you want."

"Okay, that's cool. Just call me later if you can pry yourself away from your maaaaaannn," I joked.

Genie and I laughed then she hurriedly got off the phone. I couldn't understand why I couldn't have found love with Malik like Genie and Erik had done in each other whether they wanted to admit it or not.

While Sarina was doing my nails, I got an incoming call from an unknown number. Usually, I wouldn't answer unknown calls, but whoever it was wouldn't let up and kept calling back to back.

"Hello–"

"Hello, you have a collect call from an inmate at the Glenview Police Department named, 'Malik'," I heard Malik's voice cutting into the greeting. "Will you accept the charges? Press one for yes and two for no."

Pressing one my heart dropped hearing that Malik was in jail.

"Hello, hello Chantel," Malik said before I could say anything.

"Malik, why are you calling me from jail?" I asked.

"Because I'm locked up Chantel, why do you think?!"

"What's going on?"

"I need you to do me a favor."

"Oh, so you need me now. Funny how the tables turn…"

"Are you going to help me or not?" Malik asked, cutting me off.

"I don't know. It depends on what you need."

"I'm waiting to get processed to see what my bail will be. Once I make bail, can you bond me out and I'll give the money right back to you?"

"What did you get arrested for?"

"Chantel why does that matter? Are you going to help me or what?"

"Why are you calling me and not your girlfriend? Come to think of it, y'all was all lovey-dovey the other day now you need me to get you out of a bind. What did you do Malik?"

"Look, are you going to help me or not? I tried calling Erik, but he isn't answering the phone. Had he answered, I wouldn't have bothered you."

"Oh, so, I'm your last resort?"

"Chantel it's either a yes or no?"

"What do I get out of it if I chose to help you?"

"You have three minutes left," the operator interrupted.

"Come on Chantel! Look, I'm sorry for everything that happened between us. Now can you do me this one solid? Please?!"

"I'll think about it, Malik. Call me back when you get bail."

The call disconnected before Malik could respond. I didn't know how to feel. It was confusing that he would call me instead of Grace. The only thing that I could think was that something had gone down between the two of them. But what could have happened that would lead to Malik getting arrested?

I felt conflicted because I didn't know if I should be there for Malik or not. After everything he had done to me, I wanted to put him in my past and leave him there. But that one small part that would always have a softness to him kept nagging at me.

As Sarina started on my nails, I waited to hear back from Malik. Once he made bond, I would know what he was being charged with and depending on what his charges were would determine if I would help him out or not.

# Chapter 16

### Desmond

When I asked Grace if she wanted to meet Faith and told her that my family were the ones that adopted our daughter, I expected for Grace to be emotional. What I didn't expect was for her to get up and walk away.

As I sat on the couch and waited for her to come back into the living room, I texted my dad to check in on him and to see how things were going at the hospital. I knew that the timing for everything was all off, but when was there ever a good time to tackle hard things other than head on.

After what seemed like an eternity, Grace came back and joined me in the living room.

"Look," I decided to speak up first. I could tell that she was emotional. "I didn't mean to come over here and upset you. I know that this is a lot and the timing sucks but ever since I saw you the first time a while back, I have thought about this day. Then when my mom passed and made it a point to tell Faith and me to find you, I knew that I had to fulfill that promise."

"Why now though? If your family has had her all this time, why are you just telling me now?"

"It's a complicated situation Grace, you know that. We were instructed by the adoption agency to not reach out, otherwise it could jeopardize the adoption. We didn't want to take the chance at losing Faith, so before seeing you, I never thought about it."

"Why now though? I get that your mom wanted me to know. But had she not gotten ill, would she have still wanted me to know?"

"I don't know Grace and I can't ask her that now. I will say that if there ever was a plan it was to wait until Faith got much older and explained it all to her. I will be honest in saying that my mom getting sick played a very big part in me telling you now."

"I see." Grace cried.

I felt so bad for being the reason behind all of the pain that was going on in her life.

"I'm sorry Grace. Imagine how it was for me. I had to walk around our daughter and pretend to be her older brother."

"But you got to be around her Desmond. You can't compare that to how I have been feeling."

"I didn't have a way to contact you. You mom disconnected your number when you left."

"How did you find me now though?"

"My dad got me your information actually. It seems that he and your dad kept in contact with each other throughout the years."

Grace sat there with an unreadable expression on her face.

"Long story short, when my mom passed, my dad reached out to your dad and spoke to your stepmom. That's when we found out your dad passed... my condolences. Sorry for your loss Grace."

"This is all just a lot."

"I know it is Grace. So, you still haven't answered my question. Do you want to meet our daughter Faith, Grace?"

"Yes! Of course, I want to meet her," Grace cried.

I got up and sat next to her on the couch and gave her a slight hug. Taking out my phone, I texted my dad the address and directions so that he could bring Faith over to meet Grace.

"I look a mess. Maybe she shouldn't see me like this."

"You look beautiful Grace," I assured her to ease her mind.

She went upstairs to let Kim know and to freshen up. Her bruises were bad, but not like they were yesterday when I saw her. I guess the makeup she mentioned had helped to cover it up.

When my dad told me that he was outside, I got up to go out and meet him Faith.

"Hey Faithy, how was Ace and Lexi?"

"Hey Dessy, they were fine. Lexi let me hold Ace."

"She did! You are going to be the best big sister any lil brother can ask for." I tickled her to lighten the move. "So, I have a surprise for you."

"Is that why we are over here?" Faith asked.

"Yep, it sure is. I swear you are one smart kid."

"What's the surprise?"

"Remember we talked about you meeting Grace?" I asked.

"My real mom Grace?"

"Yeah, that Grace. Would you like to still meet her?"

"Yes, I want to see what she looks like."

"Are you sure you are ready? Because she is inside of that house right now. If you're not ready, we can come back at a different time. But if you are ready, you can come with me and I'll take you to meet her right now."

Taking Faith by the hand I led her into the house so that she could meet Grace. My dad decided to wait in the car. He felt that this was a moment that the three of us needed to have alone.

When I walked up to the door, I knocked before I walked in. It was just common courtesy to knock before walking up in someone's house even though I was just in there.

As soon as we stepped into the doorway, Grace was standing there, while Kim and Andre were standing on the landing upstairs looking down at us.

Faith looked up at Grace as she tightly squeezed my hand.

"Faith, this is Grace. Grace, this is Faith Lynn," I said introducing my daughter to her mom.

Grace slowly walked up to Faith, then wrapped her arms around her and gave her a hug. Faith hugged her back and I was thankful for that. I wasn't sure how Faith was going to react seeing Grace, but they both took it pretty good.

As Grace and Faith headed into the living room, Kim and Andre came downstairs to meet Faith and I went to go get my dad. I needed to head back up to the hospital. The last thing that I needed was for Lexi to start flipping out.

I decided to send Lexi a text letting her know that I would be up there in a little while. Surprisingly, she was okay with it because she had her mom visiting with her. Me, my dad and Faith ended up staying for a few more hours than planned to meet up this week for dinner.

It had been over a decade since Grace saw our daughter and the reunion between the two of them was very special and emotional for us all. I was very thankful that everything went okay because I wasn't sure how this would go. The look on Faith's face when she first saw Grace was priceless, as was the look on Grace's face when she saw Faith.

I knew that this was only the beginning, but I felt like we were on a great start to something very good.

### Later That Evening

Making it back up to the hospital, I couldn't help but to feel complete for the first time since losing my mom. My son was born, me and Faith got reunited with Grace; things were really starting to look up. Now, I just needed to tackle the hardest part of all and that was to talk to Lexi about everything.

Making it to her room, I took a deep breath and prayed that her mom was gone so that Lexi and I could talk and two, for Lexi to not act a fool.

"Sssssss, I just got him to sleep. Please don't wake him."

I had stopped at the gift shop and brought her some flowers and candy. I forgot to bring her something to eat. I had a bit much going on all day.

"Are you hungry? I can run down to get you something from the cafeteria?" I asked as I stepped further into the room.

Peeking into the bassinet that my son was sleeping in, I rubbed the side of his cheek then took a seat next to Lexi on her bed.

"What took you so long to come back up here?"

"I had to take care of something important?"

"What could be more important than being up here with your son?"

"Lexi we gotta talk about something," I began as she gave me a weird look. "Now that my son is here and we all are family, there is something that I need to tell you that only my family knows."

"Okay, what is?" Lexi asked.

"Faith is really my daughter, not my sister."

"What?!"

"My parents adopted her when she was born."

"How come you never told me this?"

"Because there wasn't a reason for me to tell you. I'm telling you now because she is our son's big sister. She knows so it only makes sense that you should know as well."

"I'm speechless. What other family secrets do you have that I should know about?"

"That is the only 'secret' in my family. Faith's adoption was a closed adoption, so it's not something that we as a family went around telling everyone."

"Wow! I never knew. I understand where you're coming from though. Who is Faith's mom? Where has she been all these years?"

"Her mom was sent away by her mother right after our daughter was born. She just recently moved back and just met Faith for the first time since she delivered her."

"Wait a minute... who is the chick? Is that where you have been all day?"

"Her name is Grace."

"Grace...Grace... hold up! Is she the chick you saw at the restaurant that day?"

"Something like that."

"I knew something was up with you and her. The way y'all were looking at each other all makes sense to me now. Wow! So, are you and her back together? Is that where you were instead of being here with us?"

"Look Lexi, I don't want to argue with you about this. Everything that is going on is all new to me, so cut me a little slack. I'm here now and I'm being honest and telling you what is going on. You should be understanding if nothing else."

"I am trying to be understanding. I guess I'm just trying to figure out why you couldn't be here for us and all of that couldn't be put on hold. At least until I'm discharged."

"For one, everything doesn't revolve around you Lexi. Yes, you just had our son, but I knew that you were straight. Plus, you had company throughout the day. Faith meeting her mom was about Faith, my other child. A lot is changing for her right now. Losing my mom, becoming a big sister and now meeting her real mom is a lot for a 10- year old girl."

After a few minutes of silence, she surprised me when with what she did next. I guess Lexi needed to take everything in.

"Well for what it's worth, I appreciate and respect you for telling me all of this. Now that I know, I will make sure that Faith gets to spend all the time she wants with Ace."

"I appreciate you for being understanding."

I stayed until Lexi got ready for bed then headed home so that I can check in on Faith and my dad.

# Chapter 17

### Malik

I couldn't believe that I had gotten arrested after I was the one that got jumped on by dude at the hospital. Then for it to be because Grace had called and reported me to the law really had me feeling some type of way. I specifically told her to keep the law out of it. I guess that was the reason why she had me blocked from calling her.

I remember specifically telling her to not say anything, but she went behind my back and did it anyway. I didn't know what was going on with the women I had let into my life lately. Lauren had done lost her mind inviting me over then having a thug up in her shit, Chantel and the whole baby mess and now Grace.

When I got to the police station and was booked, I figured that once I was processed, I would be given a bond. When I called Chantel, it was only because Erik hadn't answered my calls. Knowing him, he was probably laid up with one of his ho's. Chantel was my last resort and she had the nerve to wanna give me grief about helping me out. All I wanted to do was to make sure that I had someone here to bond me out as soon as my bail was posted.

When the phone disconnected, all I could think was if she didn't help me that would make her one selfish bitch. As I sat in intake and watched as a drunk lady was brought in and processed, all I could think about was why Grace would do this to me. All I wanted was for her to keep it real with me, but from day one that was something that she seemed to have a hard time doing. Now that she got me arrested, in addition to me getting into with her ex, I was strongly thinking about leaving her ass alone. I was tired of having to fight and defend myself to dudes because women couldn't keep it real.

I had planned to go see Grace, despite all that bullshit that ex of hers had spat. I was going to give her a piece of my mind as soon as I got out of the hospital, but the police came and changed all of that.

"So, Mr. Wallace, did you know that you had outstanding warrants?" one of the police officers asked me.

He had taken me into a small room where I was supposed to be getting an update on my charges. I thought it was to discuss my bond. That wasn't the case though.

"Outstanding warrants for what? I don't have no outstanding warrants."

"You have outstanding warrants for two previous domestic charges for failure to appear in court. This makes it your third domestic, and that is not good for you."

"My third domestic! That's bullshit! And those other warrants are bullshit too! I was told that if I didn't show up to court the charges were gonna get dropped. My ex said that she wasn't going to show up and that if I didn't show up either, the case would have been automatically dropped!" I spat.

The previous domestics that he was talking about were from a long time ago. I didn't even talk to my ex anymore, nor had I seen her in ages. As far as I was concerned, those cases she put on me were dismissed. She had called and told me that she wasn't going to go to court and that if I didn't go, the judge would just throw it out. Now, I was finding out that wasn't the case. How was it that it took this long for those old charges to catch up to me? If Grace would have kept the law out of it like I told her ass, none of this would be happening to me.

"It's most definitely not bullshit. What's bullshit is you thinking you didn't have to go to court."

"Like I said, I was told not to show up! If I had I known that wasn't the case, I would have gone to court."

"Well, it's too late for that now."

"I swear, all you people want to do is keep a good man down."

"How so when it's your actions that landed you in jail?"

"Can you just tell me how much my bond is so that I can call and have someone get me out of this nasty ass place? I'm not a criminal, jail ain't for me."

"Well, you might as well get used to it here 'cause you won't be getting a bond. Right now, you're not eligible to make a bond."

"Why the fuck not?"

"You have to go before the judge and since today is Sunday, that can't happen until tomorrow."

"So, what are you saying? I can't get a bond today?"

"No, you won't be getting a bond today and you'll be lucky if you get one when you go before the judge. These new charges are being filed as a felony charge. So, I'm saying, just so that you are clear, you're going to be spending quite a few nights with us. You might as well make yourself comfortable."

"A felony?! I'm no felon! How is a little domestic dispute considered a felon?"

"It's based off the severity of the crime and injuries sustained by the victim. According to the report that was taken at the hospital, you did quite a bit of damage to the victim."

"Victim?! You make it seem like I killed someone. Grace isn't a victim! We had a little dispute, but there wasn't any major damage done to her. That cut on her head is because she tripped and fell! That was on her not me! As far as I know, that was all that was wrong with her."

"Well, the report says different."

"I know this some bullshit! Is this how you people treat the citizens in this town?! I was just in the hospital and you want to keep me in jail overnight! That's fucked up. What about my pain medication? I have broken ribs and need my pain pills."

"Welp, this is jail Mr. Wallace, you don't get to have narcotics in jail. The nurse will come check in on you and she will be able to give you something for the pain."

I couldn't believe my ears. All because of Grace I now had to sit in jail and pray that the judge saw my side in all of this and let me post bond. As far as those other warrants, I was confident that those would be thrown out once the judge saw how long ago they were and that my ex wasn't actively pressing the issue because we both had moved on.

I was allowed to make another phone call, so I tried to reach out to Erik again, but he still didn't answer. That shit was annoying as hell. Here I was in a real-life emergency and his ass couldn't answer the damn phone. Taking my chances, I called Chantel again and prayed that not only she answered, but that she would have changed her mind and was willing to help me out.

"Hello, you have a collect call from an inmate at the Glenview Police Department named, 'Malik'," I said as I crossed my fingers hoping she would accept the call. "Will you accept the charges? Press one for yes and two for no."

"Hello Chantel, you there?"

"Yes Malik, I'm here."

"I need a favor," I began as I heard Chantel breathe out heavily. "They are saying that I might not get to post bond. Can you please come to the courthouse tomorrow? Just in case the judge lets me post bond so you can bond me out? I promise I will make this all up to you. Just please do this for me."

"I don't know Malik."

"I know tomorrow is Monday but please, I promise I won't ask you for nothing else. And, I will even support you during the pregnancy."

"I guess I'll just tell you now since you obviously won't be going to work tomorrow. I left you a note on your desk at the job. I no longer work there, and I miscarried the baby Malik. So now, you don't have to make me any promises that I know you not gone keep."

"I'm sorry you miscarried the baby Chantel," I lied. "And since when did you stop working there? You were at work on Friday."

"Friday was my last day. Like I told you earlier, why don't you call your girlfriend to go to court for you. I don't want nothing else to do with you Malik. Please stop calling my phone. I will not be accepting any more of your collect jailhouse calls."

CLICK!

I know that bitch did not just hang up on me again. Wow! Chantel was so out of pocket for that shit. The only good news I got out of that conversation was that she no longer worked at Kraft, so I wouldn't have to see her face any more at work. Oh, and let me not forget that she lost the baby.

Hanging up the phone, I couldn't do anything but sit and wait. My body was aching, my stomach was empty, and because of Grace's ass I was stuck in fucking jail.

# Epilogue

## One Year Later
### Chantel

Over the last year, so much had changed in my life. After getting Malik out of my system, I was able to focus on me. When he asked me to show up to court for him, I battled with myself for a whole day on whether or not I should show up. I decided to go, not because I had planned on bonding him out, but because I wanted to be nosey. I wasn't working at the time, so I figured what the hell.

*When Malik walked into the courtroom, his face lit up when he saw me. I knew that he was trying to get in contact with Erik and if I wanted to, I could have called Genie because I knew that she was with Erik. She could have told him what was going on with Malik, but I didn't feel like it.*

*Malik had done me so bogus that I was relishing in the fact that karma had caught up to his ass. I assumed that he was going to make bond and go back to his fucked up ways, so imagine my surprise when that wasn't the case.*

*When the judge got in his ass for being violent against women, I was shocked that he had such a past. He choked me that one time, but I had no clue that he had a history of being violent with women. Finding out his history of domestic violence made it easy for me to move on and get him out of my system.*

*When the judge went into detail about the injuries he had given to Grace and how he was being charged with a felony, I instantly felt sick to my stomach. Although I didn't like Grace and I had given her hell about Malik, she didn't deserve for him to beat on her. Now, I knew why he was calling on me for help and not Grace.*

*When court was over, I headed home and started my job search. It took me a little over a month to get another job and lucky for me, my new job paid more than I was getting paid at Kraft.*

Since my new job wasn't that far from Kraft, Genie and I still met up for lunch a couple of times a week. She and Erik had finally come out as a couple and from what she had told me, things were going really good for them. They lived together now and let her tell it, she claimed that they were on the road to getting engaged. She was just waiting on him to pop the big question to her.

As for me, since I was no longer focused on Grace and Malik, I took the extra time to work on myself. It took me a couple of months, but I pulled up my big girl panties and ended up reaching out to Grace to extend an olive branch to her.

I was glad that phone call went well because I didn't want to have any bad karma coming back to me for the way that I had treated her. I remembered how surprised Grace was when I called her.

*"Hello Grace, this is Chantel."*

*"Hey Chantel, why are you calling me?"*

*"Do you have a second to talk?"*

*"If this is about Malik, he and I are no longer together so if you're calling to start some shit about him you can save yourself the drama."*

*"It's about him, but I'm not calling to start anything with you. I would have had this conversation in person but since I no longer work at Kraft, I opted to call. I just want to say that I am sorry for all of the trouble that I caused you because of Malik. He is a sack of shit and wasn't worth all the drama that I was starting up over him. I was just in my feelings when he started dating you because he and I were still sleeping together and of course, because of the pregnancy. After losing the baby and seeing Malik for who he really is, I feel stupid for the way that I treated you. I just wanted to be the bigger person and apologize to you."*

*"I understand and you're right, you were being very stupid,"* Grace responded. *I wanted to snap on her, but since she took the time to hear me out, I figured the least I could do was let say whatever she needed. "I'm sorry you lost your*

baby. I know what that feels like and I don't wish that kind of hurt and pain on anyone, friend or foe."

"Thanks Grace, I appreciate you for saying that. Sorry you suffered the loss of a child as well. I feel really bad for how I treated you. It wasn't cool of me to act that way toward you when you didn't do anything to me. My frustrations were with Malik."

"I'm glad you understand that because you should have kept whatever y'all had between y'all. I get it though. I get why you were upset. You just went about it wrong. I appreciate your apology though."

"Thanks. Oh, and I have one more thing to say. Malik reached out to me when he got arrested for putting his hands on you and I went to his court hearing. When I heard what he did to you, I was instantly disgusted. Sorry you had to go through that. No man should ever put his hands on a woman. I have major respect for you for standing up for yourself and having him arrested."

"Thanks Chantel, I appreciate that. Well, I actually have company over, so I have to go. Thanks again for the call."

Hanging up from Grace that day really changed how I went about things moving forward with men. I told myself that moving forward if I were to ever find myself in a similar situation again, I would never address the female because I was wrong for that. The whole time I was hating on what I thought she had with

Malik when he was putting her through just as much hell as he had put me through. The only difference was he wasn't beating on me.

I guess in a small way, her coming into his life saved me from ultimately getting beat by him, especially since he had a history of hitting on women.

As far as love goes for me, I was currently dating two different guys at the moment and I must say that I was fine with not being in an exclusive relationship. When and if that time came for me to settle down, I just prayed that God sent me the man that was for me. Until then, I planned to enjoy life, be happy and get to the money.

### Malik

Never in a million years did I think that I would get sentenced to 18 months in jail. The judge that I had was a female of course, and she must have had her panties in a bunch that morning because she showed me no mercy. I didn't think it was fair that my old cases from my ex were taken into consideration and it was fucked up for Grace to report.

It was bad enough that she sent her ex after me, but then to have me locked was just overkill in my opinion. I ended up losing my job behind all that mess and the one lesson that I took from it was to make better decisions on the women all allowed into my life.

I had a bad habit of picking women that weren't worthy of my time and who loved to test me and push me over the edge, forcing my bad side to surface.

I was hoping that Grace would have shown up to my court dates being that it was her fault that I got locked up, but she didn't show. Had she shown up, I would have been able to talk her into dropping the against me and I more than likely wouldn't have had to serve any time. Being that it was my third time getting arrested for the same thing, the judge chose me to make an example out of.

What I didn't expect was for Chantel to show up. It was like she only came to make a mockery of me. When I tried to make eye contact with her, she wouldn't even look my way. By the time I got in contact with Erik, it was too late. There was nothing that he could do for me because the judge didn't let me post a bond.

I only had a couple of months left until I was set free and I couldn't wait to get my life back on track. Initially, I planned to see Grace once I got out, but after thinking about it, it would probably be best if I just let her be. I was sure that she and her ex were probably out in the world living the good life while I had been locked up. Being that she liked to get the law involved, I knew it would not be worth the risk to fuck around with her again.

The judge made it a point and I heard her loud and clear when she said that the next time if I were to get arrested she would personally see to it that I would have to serve triple the time she gave me. 18 months had been long enough to be locked away in a cage.

I wasn't the type that was built for jail. It was dirty, it stunk, and it was full of criminals and thugs. When I first was brought in, I tried focusing on getting better physically. It took months for my ribs to heal and I still had pain from time to time. The pain medication that they were giving me didn't help because they didn't give me enough of it.

It had been nothing but torture being locked up with broken ribs. Once I got out, I hoped to never have to spend another day in nobody's jailhouse ever again.

If it weren't for Janice, who was a corrections officer for the nightshift looking out for me, my stay would have been a lot worse. When she made it known that she was feeling me, I played on her emotions and as a result, she made sure that I was good, at least during the shifts that she worked.

Once I was released, she and I planned on seeing where things went. I was looking forward to chilling with her, because more than likely I was going to need a place a stay and someone to help me out being that I was now jobless with a felony on my record.

I just hoped that with my record, I'd be able to find work. Otherwise, I was fucked.

## Desmond

Things had been going pretty good over the last year. My dad was doing good and had even entertained the idea of dating. He still said that my mom was his one true love and that he would never be able to love another woman as much as he loved her, but the new lady in his life made him happy.

He started dating Grace's stepmom a few months ago and had been out to Vegas to visit her a few times. At first, I wasn't sure how I would feel about my dad dating. It took me a while to get over it, but now I was happy for him. Grace's stepmom Sabrina came to visit Grace after her and Faith connected. She wanted to meet Faith and to check in on Grace. During that visit, Sabrina spent a lot of time with us and that was how she and my dad ended up hooking up.

I knew he was seeing her more for companionship because I know he missed having my mom around. The last thing that I wanted was for my dad to be lonely, so I was in full support of him and Sabrina.

My son was growing up fast and he and Faith were very close. When he was first born, Faith was a little jealous of him because he got a lot of attention being that he was baby. But with Grace in her life, she eventually got used to being a big sister and now they were inseparable.

As for Lexi and me, we had been doing a really good job co-parenting. When I first told her about Faith being my daughter, she really didn't handle it well, but eventually she got over it and we had been fine ever since. I would be lying if I said that it had been a smooth road co-parenting with her because every now and then, Lexi would have an outburst over something silly but for the most part we had come a long way.

When Grace and I started dating, Lexi tried giving me hell about seeing Ace. Once she started dating the guy that she was with now, she eased up on giving me hell and I was thankful that she finally moved on. I believed that she was hoping to eventually get back together with me since all we used to do was break up and get back together, but once Grace came back into my life there was no turning back for me.

The day that Grace was reunited with Faith was a day that I'd never forget. My mom was right, no matter how much my dad and I made it a point to look out for and care for Faith, she still needed motherly love.

I was surprised at how fast Faith opened up to Grace. It was natural, genuine and a blessing to see the two of them back together again.

Grace and I ended up becoming really good friends and over time, it was like our souls reconnected and once she was ready, we decided to give love another try. I was glad that she was open to love especially after everything that she had gone through with her ex. He ended up having to spend some time in jail for what he did to her and it was the best thing that could have happened. I was worried at first that dude was going to be a problem and that I was going to have to ruff him up again, but now, he had become a non- factor in Grace's life.

It took her some months to get over him and all that she went through while she was with him. I believed that if it weren't for her friend Kim and her stepmom Sabrina, she probably would have been more guarded with me. But with them encouraging her to give us a try again, I really felt that it made a difference and for that, I would always be indebted to Sabrina and Kim.

As for me and Grace, I planned to love on her and treat her the way that she deserved to be treated as we caught up on all the time that we missed out on as a family. I never thought that I would say this, but this was the happiest I had been in a long time. I didn't think that I would be able to move forward after my mom died and pick up where she left off with raising Faith. I knew that me and my dad would have figured things out along the way but having Grace in our lives had truly been a game changer. We were happy, blessed and in love... again.

## Grace

The past year had been nothing short of a whirlwind. My biggest lesson was Malik. Never would I have ever thought that I would be in a domestic violence relationship. When I first met Malik I was guarded, gullible and scared to love. The moment I opened up to him, he showed just why I was having those vibes.

I should have gone with my intuition and never gotten involved with him. The moment that I fell for him, he did just what I feared, which was hurt me. The only difference was his hurt came in the form of both emotional and physical pain.

When he jumped on me the last time, I was terrified to get the police involved, but I never regretted my decision. The lawyer had told me that I didn't have to show up to court if I was not comfortable going and even though Desmond told me that he would go with me for support, I wasn't ready to face Malik so I chose to not go. My lawyer told me that whether I went or not, since it was a domestic violence case the state would pick it up. And being that he had two previous domestic violence charges that he failed to show up to court for, he ended up having to fight all three cases. When the judge ordered for him to serve 18 months in jail, I was shocked. I honestly didn't expect for him to have to stay in jail. I thought that at worst he would have to pay to get out of jail then get hit with a ton of fines.

One of the biggest fears that I had was that Malik was going to get out of jail and come looking for me, but I hadn't had to worry about that for the last year. Now, with his time in jail was coming to an end, I still didn't worry about him because with Desmond in my life, letting it be known to Malik that he wasn't afraid of him, I didn't think I had anything to worry about.

Things at my job were going great. I was relieved that Malik got fired, so once he did get out of jail, I wouldn't have to worry about him coming back to Kraft to work. What really shocked me was Chantel quitting. That was something that was totally unexpected.

Then when Chantel called me and apologized, I was one hundred percent not expecting that. Chantel had a deep hatred for me. You could have seen it in her eyes whenever she would look at me. Her eyes were filled with anger and hate. So, for her to call me and apologize really made me feel good.

I couldn't understand why she was so angry with me, being disrespectful and all at work which was totally inappropriate on her part. She should have been directing all of her anger toward Malik. I now knew that I was an easy target for her. Hopefully, she learned from all of that to never act like that again. I was just happy to be done with Malik and his abusive hands, and Chantel and all of her mess.

Now that she didn't work at Kraft anymore, Genie and I had become pretty cool. We didn't hang out outside of work, but we were cool and we chit chatted every now and then, which was much better than how things were when Chantel was there. The atmosphere at work was so much better now without Chantel and Malik there.

Seeing my mom the day that Malik jumped on me actually gave me more closure than I expected it would. To say that I was not prepared to see my mom would be an understatement. What hurt the most was the fact that even though it was over a decade since the last time we had seen each other, she picked up right where we had left it. She still treated me like shit. There was a small part of me that wished that she would have acted like a mother and showed me some kind of love and affection. I had to learn the hard way that that was just something that she would never be capable of doing.

Whatever issues my mom had with me were just that, her issues. Since then I learned to deal with the fact that she and I would never have a mother daughter relationship and I was okay with that. The relationship that I had with my stepmom Sabrina was a blessing and even though she wasn't my birth mother, she showed me the love that my mom was not able to give me, and I was cool with that.

Kim had been a true angel in my life. She had become the big sister that I never had and didn't realize that I needed. She and Dre were inseparable still going strong with plans to get married soon. Over this last year, Kim had gotten to spend a lot of time with Faith and she was now ready to start a family of her own.

Me and Desmond went out on double dates regularly with Kim and Dre. I'd be the first to admit that if it weren't for Kim and Sabrina, I probably wouldn't have given Desmond and I a chance. I wasn't sure how I felt about his ex, Lexi. The last thing that I needed was to go through any drama with a female over a man like I had to do with Chantel and Malik. Thankfully, Lexi wasn't anything like Chantel and in the end, everything ended up working out.

The best thing that had happened to me was that my daughter was back in my life, as well as Desmond. When he told me that his family adopted Faith, I wasn't sure how I should feel. At first, I was upset and even in some ways jealous because he had the opportunity to watch Faith grow. Then, after the shock of it all, I was relieved that his family adopted her because had she gone to live with someone else, I probably wouldn't have had the opportunity to have her in my life now.

When I saw Faith for the first time, my heart opened in a way that I never thought that it would. My biggest fear was that she wouldn't want to meet me or that she would be upset with me for giving her up. Thankfully, that wasn't the case. Faith was a lot more understanding than I thought she would be, and I had Desmond and his family to thank for that.

I wondered all the time if Desmond's mom was still alive if she would have been okay with me being in Faith's life. That was something that I thought about often. I hated that she had to get sick and pass away, but I felt like everything happened for a reason. As the saying goes, we're not supposed to question God. I was very grateful to have my daughter and Desmond back in my life and I looked forward to our journey together.

## The End

# NOTE TO MY READERS:

If you're reading this note that means you made it to the end of the finale and for that, I am truly appreciative. Thanks for taking this emotional rollercoaster ride with me and these characters.

Malik is proof that there are men that live to prey on women that are vulnerable. And Grace proved that there are some women that experience so much pain that it takes them a minute to gather enough strength to move on.

I hope that Grace's journey of strength, love and growth helps to encourage any woman who may have read this story that is in a similar situation.

This story isn't to show women in a weak essence, but to give some insight into why we as women sometimes have to weather a storm to become strong.

Violence whether in the form of emotional or physical abuse is never okay. Loving someone and being loved by someone should NEVER be painful. If you or someone you know is in an abusive relationship, I encourage you to please get help. Call the Domestic Violence Hotline at 800-799-SAFE (800-799-7233) someone is available 24/7 to answer and assist you.

I would love to know if you enjoyed this series. My hope is that you did. I encourage you to please leave a review on Amazon. I would love to know your feedback.

Thanks again,

Love & Kisses,

~Loryn

CPSIA information can be obtained
at www.ICGtesting.com
Printed in the USA
LVHW041948061120
670968LV00003B/418